MURDER, MYSTERY & DATING MAYHEM

By D.E. HAGGERTY

Dedication

To all the women who have survived turning 40 and managed to come out on the other side unscathed or perhaps just a tiny bit scathed, but all the stronger for it

Chapter 1

"Middle of the Road" – The Pretenders

"Ugh!" I shout at the mirror and throw my eyebrow tweezers at it. Expecting a loud thunk but only getting a little ping instead, annoys me further. Growing old sucks balls and not just any balls – big, hairy, sweaty balls. I can handle the wrinkles. Everyone gets wrinkles. I can even handle the gray hair. After all, it can look dignified or, more likely, be dyed back to its original color when all else fails. But dark hairs on my chin? That's where I draw the line.

I hear a laugh behind me and look to see Jack staring at me with mirth in his eyes. I should have never given the man a key to my house. Jack is my BFF and has been since the first day of middle school. Some kid called me metal mouth and before I had a chance to smack him, which I totally would have, Jack came to my rescue. We've been inseparable ever since. When Jack *came out* to his parents, I was the one standing next to him holding his hand. He slept on the floor of my bedroom at my parents' house for a month until his own calmed down.

Just because Jack is my BFF doesn't mean I don't get embarrassed when he catches me trying to rid myself of evidence that I am aging and much faster than him at that. Jack's my age, but he looks at least a decade younger. Life is so freaking unfair!

"Put down your weapons," Jack says and raises his hands in surrender.

"Ha, flipping ha," I mutter. I narrow my eyes when I catch sight of a pink flyer in his hands. *Oh no.* My BFF is the king of harebrained schemes, and a pink flyer can only mean bad news. I start to back away but have nowhere to go in my tiny bathroom.

Jack smiles and starts stalking me like a predator. He waves the flyer at me. He actually bounces on his toes in excitement. "I signed you up for speed dating!" Speed dating? Also known as – how can I embarrass myself over and over in a single evening?

I stop moving backward, cross my arms across my chest and plant my feet. "You did what!" I may have shrieked.

Jack's smile turns into a smirk.

"I'm not going," I announce and try to push past him.

Jack is having none of that. He grips my elbow, stopping me. "Oh yes you are missy! You're going or I'm going to tell everyone about your little chin hair problem."

I gasp. "You wouldn't!" He doesn't respond but continues to smirk at me. Shoot, he totally would. The little creep! I drop my face into my hands and whine. "Why? Why are you doing this to me?"

Jack throws his head back and laughs. "Seriously?" He raises one eyebrow at me. "You need to get laid woman!"

It's annoying how Jack is almost always right. I do indeed need to get laid. I recently turned forty, and I've been a widow for almost five years. I've tried getting back in the game a few times, but I'm just not that interested. Okay, I lie. I'm totally interested, but the dates I've suffered through since losing my husband were disasters of such epic proportions, I gave up.

I blame myself. I have no idea how to date. Ryan, my late husband, was my first and only boyfriend, and then I married him. We met in college and it's not like dating is something you do in college, or at least I didn't. Ryan and I just hung out together watching movies and having drinks at the bar with other friends. At some point, he started calling me his girlfriend and that was that. We married straight out of college and then he died when I was thirty-five. Going on your first date at the age of thirty-six is not fun, let me tell you. I'm awkward at the best of times. On a date, when I'm nervous, I'm a downright disaster. Speed dating can't be any worse, I guess.

"Fine," I groan. "When is it?"

"Tonight." He mutters and then starts to back out of the room before turning tail and full-out running away.

"What?" I shout as I chase after him. I catch up to him and grab the flyer. He's got some nerve. And then a brilliant idea hits me. I cross my arms and go on the attack. "If I have to go, then you're going with me."

Jack's laughter immediately stops. It's his turn to cross his arms. He looks down from his six-foot-three-inch towering height and raises an eyebrow at me. "And, pray tell, who am I going to meet at this affair?" In case I miss his meaning, he adds a whole lot of diva to his voice.

"I don't care," I shrug. "But I'm not going alone and that's final."

"Fine," Jack huffs and stalks off. "I'll pick you up at 6," he yells through the screen door.

Three hours later I've managed to rid my chin of any hairy evidence and cleaned myself up reasonably well. Since I don't usually wear make-up, I suck, like majorly, at putting it on, but the bags under my eyes aren't going to disappear on their own. Puffy eyes are testimony of an afternoon spent staring at my computer screen working on Jack's website. As a freelance graphic designer, I have to grab every assignment that I can. But even if I didn't need to take every job that comes my way, this is Jack we're talking about. I'd do anything for the man – even humiliate myself at a speed dating event – and he knows it.

I put down the eyeliner pencil and have a look at the results. For a middle-aged woman, I don't look entirely unfortunate. Even though I workout like the devil possessed, I'm slightly overweight but at a height of five-eight, I can carry a bit of extra weight. Fortunately, for me, most of my weight falls into the tits and ass categories. My hair is curly, brown, and currently long. I hope my long eyelashes and sparkly green eyes distract from the wrinkles around my eyes.

The doorbell rings and halts my perusal of my looks. I grab my bag and jacket from the bed and head to the front door. Jack's already standing inside. He only rang the doorbell to make sure I got a move on.

"Damn girl, you look hot!" He exclaims as I reach up on tippy toes to kiss his cheek.

"You know," I say as we head out the door to Jack's car. "If you just played for the other team, we could get together and wouldn't have to do the stupid speed dating thing."

Jack laughs as he opens his car door for me. "We tried that, remember?"

Why does Jack have to remind me? At the start of high school, I forced Jack to take me to the homecoming dance. Even though he had yet to come out, he was already pretty comfortable with being gay, but I had convinced myself I was in love with my best friend. After the dance, I kissed him on the mouth. His reaction? He yelled "yuck!" and wiped his mouth. It took a month of schmoozing before I would talk to the handsome, gay guy again.

Chapter 2

"Let's Get It On" by Marvin Gaye

Speed dating is taking place at a hotel on the outskirts of our small, Nebraska town. Yes, a hotel! What exactly do the organizers expect to happen? When we arrive, I remain in the car, debating whether I'm fast enough to run back home before Jack can catch me.

"You'll never make it," Jack says and raises an eyebrow at me. Darn man! Always knows what I'm thinking.

"Fine," I huff as I get out. Jack comes around and grabs my hand. Not in a friendly way, mind you. Oh no, he's making sure I'm not going to flee.

The lobby of the hotel looks like cupid projectile vomited in it, on it, and all around it. There are red and pink balloons everywhere as well as the chubby love-god himself, in the form of a cardboard cutout, pointing us in the direction of the bar. A woman with bouffant hair sits behind a table at the entrance to the bar. She looks like she stepped out of the '50s with her puffed-out hair, overly done make-up, and plastic smile. I peek under the table to see if she's wearing a poodle skirt. Bingo!

"You must be here for the speed dating," she says with way too much enthusiasm.

Jack gives her one of his panty-dropping smiles and nods. "I'm Jack Harris and this is Izzy Archer."

Bouffant woman hands him two nametags. "You can call me Sugar. Go ahead and grab yourselves a complimentary drink. We'll be starting in a few minutes."

Jack puts his hand on the curve of my lower back and not-so-gently pushes me into the bar. I'm surprised to find the place crowded. Of course, I'm old enough to be the mother to nearly every woman there. On the other side of the sexual divide, the men attending could have fathered me. Oh, how cliché. Where are those free drinks again?

As always, Jack knows what I need and heads to a cocktail waitress holding a tray of glasses filled with red and white wine. I don't follow. There's no way I'm going to make it

5

through this evening on mere wine. They should be handing out shooters at the door. I make my way to the bar.

"Excuse me," I say as I try to catch the bartender's attention. The bartender, however, is more interested in the young girls prancing around than in me. I sigh and lean onto the bar ensuring that the girls are visible. "Excuse me," I say again, but this time I use a sultry voice – or at least that's what I'm going for. The bartender finally looks my way and I smile when I see his eyes immediately lured to my cleavage. Gotcha! "Tequila shot with a beer chaser, please." He jumps to fulfill my order, but nearly trips as he attempts to maintain eye contact with my bosom and reach for the tequila bottle at the same time.

I hear someone chuckle beside me and turn to see a hotter than hot piece of male specimen staring at me. I immediately feel my face burn. The bartender saves me by slamming my drinks down in front of me. I grab the tequila shot and quickly down it before latching onto the beer to soothe my burning esophagus. Good thing I have lots of practice or I would probably spit the beer out like a college freshman during rush week, although I may have coughed just a teensy bit.

Sufficiently fortified, I turn to the man again and notice him watching me. He raises an eyebrow. "I tried that trick earlier," he says, tilting his head towards the bar, "but the bartender didn't seem impressed with my assets." I look him up and down. "You look pretty hot to me," I say and then slap my hand over my mouth when I realize my comment probably sounded like some lame pick-up line. "Sorry." Is it possible for my face to spontaneously burst into flames? "Sometimes my mouth opens before my brain can stop it."

The man laughs and shakes his head. He reaches out to shake my hand just as a loud, obnoxious bell rings. "That's my cue," I say as I jump off the barstool. I wobble a bit, and hottie reaches out to steady me with his hand on my elbow. I gasp as a current of pure electricity moves through my arm. I startle and nearly trip in my heels.

I manage to steady myself and smile at Mr. Dreamboat before going off to search for Jack. Before I can find him, I catch sight of another cocktail waitress. I grab a glass of red before locating Jack, who is surrounded by women who are obviously on the prowl. To the casual observer, he seems to be reveling in the attention, but I see his eyes frantically search the room before landing on me. I immediately stalk forward, grab his hand, and pull him away.

Sugar, as Mrs. Enthusiastic asked us to call her, claps her hands for everyone's attention. I feel like I'm back in the classroom. Not any old classroom either, one transported back in time to when poodle skirts, puffed-up hair, and horn-rimmed glasses were popular.

"Ladies and Gentlemen," she begins after throwing a glare my way. "Welcome! Y'all are gonna have a ball tonight." I may be snickering. "On the tables are clipboards: pink for girls, blue for boys." Okay, now I'm definitely snickering. "You'll have five minutes with each date. Fill out a new questionnaire for each date. After the evening is finished, I'll collect the questionnaires. While you enjoy another drink and some socializing, I'll go over the questionnaires and let y'all know if there's a match." She claps her hands in glee. I do not roll my eyes, I swear I don't. Okay, maybe I do.

The young girls start running to the tables. I didn't know this was a race and besides my hands are full. I end up at the corner table right outside the door to the kitchen. This night just keeps getting better and better.

After the women are seated, the men each find a partner and sit down. The guy who sits down across from me doesn't seem too bad. He appears normal enough. He's not hot or anything, but he's not entirely unpleasant to look at.

Mrs. Sugar rings the bell again and we're off. The first 'date' starts off well. His name is Ed. He's not drooling or anything, is talking to me, and not my boobs, and seems to be interested in my graphic design work. Maybe Jack was right after all. I need to get myself back into the dating game.

"So," Ed begins after we've exchanged the usual pleasantries and some small talk. He leans forward and starts to whisper. "How do you feel about whips and chains?"

Not the appropriate moment to be sipping my wine, but how could I have expected that! I choke and spit a bit of wine into Ed's face, which seems to excite him. He wiggles his eyebrows. "I take it that's a yes?" he asks eagerly.

7

"Um no. That's a definite no. N.O." I lift my glass and down the remainder of my wine. The bell rings and I yell loudly "Next!"

Ed looks disappointed as he walks to the next table, but I've got my eyes on the prize. A cocktail waitress is headed my way. I snag two more glasses of wine before turning to my next date. Oh dear lord! The man is older than my grandma. He struggles to lower himself into the chair opposite mine.

There goes that annoying bell again. Time to put my game-face on. I smile and decide I'll check this guy out for Grandma. She could use a date. Although, to be perfectly honest, I don't remember her going out with a man – ever. There's no time like the present.

The old man's name is Wilbert and the five minutes pass pleasantly enough. As long as I pretend he's dating Grandma and not trying to pick me up. When the bell rings again, I rush from my chair to help Wilbert stand. I take his elbow and guide him to his next date – a girl young enough to be his great-granddaughter.

I sit back down and gather my courage for my next winner. I try to smile at the guy across from me, really I do. But have you ever tried to smile at a man with the biggest combover ever? Let me tell you, it's not easy. I may be grimacing a tiny bit.

Mr. Combover leans over and leers at me. Yes, leers at me! His eyes are surgically attached to my boobs. True, I have good boobs, but maybe pay a bit of attention to the person attached to the boobs?

Finally, done leering, he leans back and takes in my face. "You're not the youngest anymore." Really? That's the first thing Mr. Combover is going to say?

"I could say the same about you," I respond in the nasty voice I use when nagging clients who are slow to pay, but quick to make outrageous demands.

Mr. Combover clears his throat and leans in again. I bend backward as far as possible in my chair, but he's undeterred. "I'm just gonna get this out there and not waste my time." I just stare at him. "Do you put out? 'Cuz if not, I ain't got time for you."

Oh no, he didn't. "What," I sputter and grab for my first wine glass, which I down in one go. Never said I was a classy lady.

"Do. You. Put. Out?" Yes, he actually enunciates it like I didn't understand him the first time.

I'm done. I never should've come anyway. Why do I let Jack blackmail me? Other forty-year-old women have chin hair. How bad could it be if people know that I do too? I grab the second glass of wine and down it before standing up. Unfortunately, I don't have the greatest equilibrium in the best of circumstances and now is no exception. My chair crashes loudly to the floor, and I wobble on my heels a bit.

The room turns deathly quiet just before I yell, "Fuck off! I'm outta here." The young girls gasp while some of the men chuckle. I don't bother looking around to see who's chuckling and who's gasping, I flee the room. I run straight through the bar, past the lobby, and outside. I'm walking home if need be.

Luckily, Jack, the blackmailer, has my back as usual. He grabs my elbow as I start to walk toward the road and pushes me toward his car. After we're seated, he turns to me and asks, "What happened?"

I throw my hands in the air. "Mr. Combover asked if I put out!" I screech.

Jack bends over and guffaws. He laughs so hard he actually snorts and gasps for breath. I time him on the car clock – five minutes is how long it takes for him to recover. When he calms down, he pulls me in for a long hug before kissing my forehead gently and driving me home. But not before stopping for ice cream because everyone knows ice cream makes everything better.

Chapter 3

"Grandma" by Pam Feather

I wake up the next day in a much better mood than I went to bed in. Not only will Jack never take me to a speed dating event again (Yeah!), but it's also Sunday, which means I'm going to see my grandma and she totally rocks.

Grandma isn't actually my grandma, she's Ryan's paternal grandmother, but I adopted her or she adopted me – whatever. After Ryan's death nearly five years ago, Grandma and I got even closer as I didn't have to hide my visits to her from him.

Ryan's death was quite the shock, but then again, it wasn't. He died when he went parachuting and forgot to check his chute before he jumped. Some cord or thingy, which I don't really understand, was tangled and, therefore, the chute didn't open. Kerplunk! Instant widowhood for me.

That was pretty typical of Ryan. He took the word 'irresponsible' to a whole other level. He lived off my earnings, which I would have been totally okay with if he took care of the house and other crappy, boring tasks that being an adult entails. You know what I mean: paying the bills, getting the oil changed in the car, etc. But no – Ryan was too busy trying to catch his next adrenaline high and couldn't be bothered to take out the stinking trash.

I think Grandma was as frustrated with Ryan as I was. She was always nagging him. Something I eventually learned not to do because he didn't listen anyway and what fun is being a nag? He stopped going to see her to avoid her nagging, and eventually they were only strangers to one another. He absolutely missed out.

Grandma is totally awesome! Since my parents didn't approve of my match with Ryan, I haven't had much contact with my own family. Of course, it turned out that they were right about Ryan not being the best partner for me, but I was young and in love. I wasn't exactly open to listening to my parents' comments at the time. After I had realized they were right, my pride kept me from reaching out to them. Then my parents retired to Florida and the contact between us dwindled even further to calls on

Christmas, Thanksgiving, and those once-in-a-blue-moon visits. I don't have any siblings and thus Grandma eventually became my *only* family. Ryan's parents aren't alive anymore and he didn't have any siblings either. I guess, in a way, I'm the only family Grandma has as well.

I park on the street in front of Grandma's ranch house. She has a fab house set on a few acres of land on the edge of town. It has a front porch to die for – complete with swing. I covet that swing. I tease Grandma that I'm going to come over and steal it one night. She just laughs and tells me to come and use it whenever I want! She's too sweet and takes the wind out of my *stealing* sails.

The driveway is full of older, American-built cars resembling boats in size. That can only mean one thing – Grandma's hosting this week's knitting club get together. The knitting club is actually just a bunch of her closest friends who, like Grandma, are widowed and have no or few family in the area. I take a deep breath to fortify myself as I get out of my car, wondering if the ladies have started getting wild yet. It sounds like a joke, a bunch of seventy-year-olds getting out of control, but it's no lie. These women turned off their brain-to-mouth filters decades ago, and they say the darndest things – most of which makes me laugh until my stomach aches.

"Helllooo!" I yell as I walk into the house without knocking. If you want to avoid being hit by a rolling pin, you don't knock at Grandma's house. *Family doesn't knock,* she'll yell as she hits you. For an old lady, she can hit hard!

"Back here my darling girl." I follow the voice to the screened porch at the rear of the house, which has a view over the rolling hills that are part of her land. Another thing I covet about this house. Coveting isn't one of the seven deadly sins, is it? Otherwise, I'm in big trouble here.

The porch is full of elderly women knitting and babbling away. Their chattering voices halt as I enter. "Hi Izzy," they yell in unison. I smile at each of them and walk over to give Grandma a kiss on the cheek.

"Get yourself an iced tea girl, and then come sit with us."

After I get myself a drink and refill everyone else's glasses, I sit down on the footstool at Grandma's feet and start untangling some of her yarn. Grandma has arthritis in her hands, which means she doesn't knit much anymore. She needs to concentrate and doesn't gab like the other ladies. After a few minutes, she takes a break and puts down her needles with a sigh.

"Where's Jack?" she asks. I shrug in response.

"You really should marry that boy before someone else does." I snicker. We've had this conversation a million times before.

"Grandma," I explain – again. "Jack's gay."

"So he's happy. That's a good thing for a husband." I swear she's deliberately obtuse.

"Not happy. Ho-mo-sex-u-al." I speak slowly to make my point. I don't know why I bother. This is probably the billionth time we've had this conversation. Grandma is perfectly aware that Jack's gay, but she does love to tease – the old bat!

Grandma waves her hands in dismissal. "I'm sure it's just a phase. Your pretty face could convince him otherwise."

I snort, which causes grandma to give me a dirty look. *Young ladies do not snort.* Never mind that I'm not young or a lady. "I've tried that already. Trust me, it was a disaster." I can feel my face burning. Being reminded of my 'Jack humiliation' two days in a row does nothing for my self-esteem.

The other ladies agree with Grandma. "Oh, but Jack's sooo handsome." That's Betty. The ringleader of the old lady posse if there ever was one.

"I wouldn't mind trying to convince him to give the ladies a try," Rosemary chimes in.

"He can eat crackers in my bed anytime," Martha sighs with a faraway look in her eyes.

And finally Rose gives her two cents, "Such a fine pair of buttocks on him."

I laugh at the audacity of these ladies, the youngest of whom can't be a day less than seventy. Only Ally remains quiet. Not because she wouldn't take a stab at Jack should the opportunity present itself, but because she's shy when in a group.

Somehow I manage to get the topic turned to something else and spend a lovely afternoon with my favorite old ladies. That they always have lots of goodies like homemade apple pie and brownies at these gatherings has absolutely nothing to do with how enjoyable the afternoon is. Nothing at all. Yeah, that's me snorting again.

Chapter 4

"That's What Friends are For" by Dionne Warwick

My mobile phone starts to ring as I'm trying to get into my house with my hands full of plastic grocery bags. Not being the most organized of people at the best of times, there's little chance I'll locate my phone or keys before it stops ringing. Going into emergency mode, I drop the bags to conduct a search. Naturally, my groceries start to roll down the sidewalk. "Crap!"

Breathless, I finally find my phone and answer without looking at the caller ID. "What?"

Jack laughs. I growl in response. "You sound out of breath. Whatcha doing?"

I moan and kneel down to retrieve my grocery items. I tuck the phone between my ear and shoulder and grab willy-nilly at the items. "Nothing, just got home from Grandma's."

"Oh goodie!" I think I hear him clap in the background. Shit! That can't be good. "I'll be right over."

Jack never calls to tell me he's on his way. He just shows up. Jack sets his own hours and schedule as part-owner of a boutique design store downtown. The shop caters to special needs men and women. Special needs as in cross-dressers and voluptuous women. It's a one of its kind store in the region, maybe in all of Oklahoma, and people come from the surrounding counties to shop there. It's not cheap either. The store has done so incredibly well that Jack and his business partner hired a manager to run the place on a day-to-day basis. Jack only needs to physically go in once in a while although he loves to be on-hand when new clothing shipments arrive.

By the time Jack arrives, I've managed to stuff the groceries back into the bags, find my keys, open the door, and get into the kitchen. I hear the door slam and in walks Jack with a can of kidney beans in his hands. "Missing this? Or are you starting a canned bean garden?"

"Hardee har har," I respond and grab the can from him. He jumps on the counter and watches me put the groceries away. Of course, he doesn't offer to help. He is a man, after all. When he clears his throat before speaking, I know I'm in trouble.

I stop what I'm doing and assume the position – hands on hips in preparation for a fight.

Jack waves my position away. "No need to get your back up, Izzy."

Not wishing to give up entirely, I cross my arms and raise my eyebrows. I'll wait him out. He sighs. "Well, you see," he sounds almost sheepish, "I kinda, sorta arranged a date for you." He has the good sense to duck his head and stare at the ground to avoid my infuriated eyes.

"What?" I shriek. Not a pretty sound, but he – my gay best friend – did just say he arranged a date for me and, unfortunately, it wouldn't be the first time he's done this. Jack likes to set me up with men who are hiding in the closet. His words - not mine. Then he'll casually run into me during the date and try to pick the unsuspecting man up. And it works! Which is pretty annoying when the guy picked me up at my house and then takes off with Jack. I now keep a key to Jack's car on my key ring.

"Don't get your panties in a twist," Jack shouts. I growl. "This one wasn't gay." I raise my eyebrows in confusion wondering what his angle is this time. "He was at the speed dating."

My hands are back on my hips. "What? Did you see the men there?"

"Did you?"

I roll my eyes. "Which speed dating event were you at?"

"The same as you," he's glaring at me now. "Did you not see that hunk of a man sitting next to you at the bar?"

It only takes a second for Mr. Drop Dead Gorgeous' face to flash into my head. I assumed he wasn't involved in the speed dating. I mean he was more than good looking. Why would he need to go to a speed dating event? My memories catch up to my vision of the hottie, and I slap my forehead.

"Uh oh, what did you do?" Why does he assume I did something? Maybe he's right 90 percent of the time, but it's still rude to assume!

"I forgot to switch my brain on before I opened my big mouth," I mumble as I remember my words telling Mr. Hottie just exactly how hot he is.

Jack waves my concerns away. "Doesn't matter." I grunt, but he ignores me and continues. "I got his number and talked to him this afternoon. He remembers you and wants you to give him a call."

"When exactly did you get his number?"

Jack shrugs but doesn't answer. I really don't expect him to. He's always had this mysterious ability to get phone numbers from men and women for that matter.

"Wait," I shout as something occurs to me. "Did you get his number for you or for me?"

Even before Jack answers, the pink in his cheeks gives him away. "For me, so I can unequivocally say he's not gay." Hmmm… that conversation must have been awkward. Although, knowing Jack the way I do, he probably sounded smooth and debonair without even trying. So freaking unfair.

Jack reaches into his jeans and pulls out a slip of paper with a phone number and name written on it. "He's expecting your call." He sets the paper on the counter, jumps off, and leaves with a kiss to my forehead, but not before he snags the bag of caramel popcorn I'd just unpacked.

It takes me two hours and two glasses – okay three – of wine before I work up the courage to call Noel. Yes, Noel is his name. And isn't that just hot? I manage not to embarrass myself too much, I hope, and we set a date for dinner on Friday. It's only Sunday. How are my nerves going to survive until then?

Chapter 5

"Bad Moon Rising" by Creedence Clearwater Revival

On a hope and a prayer, I decide to dig out a set of sexy underwear for my date with Noel, the sexy hunk who for some strange reason was also at the speed dating event. Putting on the sexy underwear fills me with all kinds of confidence and I decide that, yes, I can wear high heels without killing myself. This date is going to totally rock!

I'm ready fifteen minutes before Noel is set to pick me up. Just enough time for a bit of liquid courage. I pour a glass of chardonnay and sit on my sofa sipping quietly while trying not to be too nervous about my date. Oh, who am I kidding? I'm gulping wine down while pacing the kitchen.

Lucky for me, and my kitchen floor, Noel is right on time. I answer the door hoping he is just as hunky as I remember – before a tequila shot, bottle of beer, and two, or was it three, glasses of wine.

"Hi!" I answer the door a bit breathlessly.

Noel smiles and extends his hand. He doesn't shake my hand when I reach out though, instead he grasps it with both of his hands and looks me directly in the eyes. "Nice to officially meet you, Izzy." I swoon a bit at that.

Noel is hotter than I remember. Go me! With my five-eight frame and wearing three inch heels, he still has to look down at me. He must be a few inches taller than six feet. I love that I can wear high heels and not tower over him. He's also a big guy. Not fat, but broad and built with wide shoulders and a muscular chest. Luckily, he's well-proportioned – no chicken legs on this one! It's clear he works out. I can see muscles bulging under his button-down shirt. His hair is dark and curls at the edges and his blue eyes sparkle with mirth as I stare at him.

"Nice to meet you too," I finally stutter in response.

Noel chuckles and releases my hand. "Ready to go?" I nod and follow him to his car after locking up.

The car stops me in my tracks. "Wow! She's a beauty." I circle the car checking out the finish on this classic baby. "Did you restore her yourself?" Ryan – aka speed junkie extraordinaire – was obsessed with muscle cars. It was one of the few obsessions of his I shared. I've always loved speed, but didn't know much about cars until Ryan. At the start of our marriage, he'd drag me to car meets all over Oklahoma and its surroundings. I soon shared Ryan's love of muscle cars. And Noel doesn't have any old muscle car but the muscle car of all muscle cars – a Pontiac GTO – one of the top ten muscle cars of all time, according to *Car and Driver* magazine.

Noel stops in his tracks and looks at me. "You know about muscle cars?"

I blush, embarrassed to be caught drooling. "I freaking love them." I shrug. "My late husband was obsessed and I caught the bug." I hear Noel's swift intake of breath, and realize I've broken date rule numero uno according to *Cosmo* – never mention a former lover, especially a dead husband. Crap.

"I'm sorry to hear about your husband," Noel sounds sincere, but I shake my head. Sure, I loved Ryan, but I fell out of love with him years before he died. I miss Ryan, the man I fell in love with, but I sure as heck don't miss the unmotivated drifter he turned into.

"Thanks," I respond. "It's okay, it's been a while." When I see Noel open his mouth, I raise my hand to forestall any further questions. "Let's not talk about it okay?" My nose wrinkles of its own accord.

Noel looks puzzled, but nods. I quickly change the subject back to the object of my lust. "So, how long have you had her?" I tilt my head to indicate the shiny, black muscle car.

"All my life. It was my dad's car."

"Seriously? He bought it from the manufacturer?" I'm even more intrigued now as I know how much money these babies are worth, especially if there has only been one owner.

Noel nods and smiles before opening the door and ushering me in. I sigh as my butt slides into the front seat. As we drive into town, he tunes the radio to a classic jazz station. I chuckle. "Is this what you normally listen to in this baby?" I don't want to sound rude, but come on, jazz and a muscle car? I'm surprised she hasn't spit us out yet.

Luckily, Noel doesn't take offense and shrugs instead. "Not really, but I didn't think hard rock was appropriate for a date."

I laugh and reach for the radio. "Seriously? My gay best friend set us up after he asked you out. I think we left appropriate behind before we began." I turn the radio to the classic metal station and dial the volume up. A song from the gods of metal, Metallica, is playing and Noel and I sing along as we drive through town.

Noel drives to a small Mexican restaurant. I turn questioning eyes on him, and he lifts his hands in surrender. "Okay, I confess! Jack told me Mexican food was your favorite." Let's just hope that's all my former bestie told Noel.

Dinner is good, maybe even awesome! I limit myself to one margarita because those things pack a punch and who knows what idiocy would flow forth from my mouth after one too many of those bad boys. Noel is an awesome guy. He's a detective on the local police force. He was worried that would bother me, but I'm not sure why. Do I look like I'm harboring guilty secrets? He explains he works long hours and gets calls at all times of the day and night. Apparently, some bitchy old girlfriends have had problems with that. (I added the bitchy part.)

But I'm not like other girls. I understand perfectly the need to work odd hours. Even if graphic design isn't as important to society as the police work Noel does, I still have to pay the bills and being self-employed means accepting nearly every assignment that comes my way and putting up with crazy deadlines from clients. And let's face it, after supporting my husband's daredevil habits, I'm just glad that Noel even has a job.

By the time dinner ends, I'm holding my breath waiting for the catch. I mean, seriously, Noel is hot, sweet, and has a job! He must be a cross-dresser or something. I consider asking him what's wrong with him, but luckily my brain and mouth are properly connected before I blurt out any stupid questions.

The waitress arrives with the check and Noel grabs it while I reach for my purse. He puts a hand on my arm. "I got it." I'm not used to men paying so I'm a bit tongue tied. "Um, thanks?" It comes out sounding like a question. I'm such a dork sometimes.

"I'm just going to go to the bathroom before we head out." I stand and grab my purse. Emboldened by a great evening, a hot guy, and one margarita, I add a bit of sway to my hips and an extra bounce to my step. And down she goes! I miss the step from the restaurant into the hallway where the restrooms are located and end up sprawled across the hallway floor. Crap on a cracker!

Of course this is the night I'm wearing a short dress that flares out and a very sexy thong. My dress is now bunched up around my waist displaying my thong for all eyes to see. A thong which doesn't even come close to covering my butt cheeks. The very same butt cheeks that are now mooning everyone in the restaurant. I think the heat from my face just lit the kitchen stove on fire.

I jump up as quickly as possible and pull my dress down before running out the back entrance of the restaurant. I'm already standing by Noel's car by the time he finds me.

"Are you okay?" He asks as he opens my door.

I nod but don't say anything. How freaking embarrassing! I don't speak on the ride home. Noel tries to start several conversations, but gives up after I only utter monosyllables in response. I jump out of the car when we reach my house. I yell thanks and goodbye before unlocking my door and slamming it behind me. Great! I finally meet a hot, nice man with a good job, and I had to totally ruin it. I'm done dating.

Chapter 6

"Friends Will be Friends" by Queen

The smell of hot cinnamon rolls and the sound of an incredibly girly shout of "Good morning! Time to rise and shine!", wake me the next morning. I peer at the alarm clock and notice it's only nine. After the most embarrassing date of the century, I tossed and turned the vast majority of the night only managing to fall asleep around three. A wake-up call at nine on Saturday is definitely not welcome.

I roll over and hide my head under the pillow. "What are you doing here at this ungodly hour?" I ask the bed.

"I heard about your little incident last night," Jack chuckles. That's right. The man actually dares to chuckle at me.

I briefly rise out of bed and throw my pillow at him. Unfortunately, my eyes are still caked shut from sleep, and I miss Jack completely. Not bothered, he giggles and bounces on the bed. "Now, now, my little padawan." He hands me a large latte and holds a cinnamon bun under my nose.

I gotta admit it, Jack knows how to win me over. I sit up and grab the offering. I take a huge bite before asking, "How did you hear?" Oh great, now I'm the talk of the freaking town!

"A hot cop called me this morning and asked me to check up on you. He was worried."

I nearly choke on my coffee. "Noel called you and told you what happened?" I stare at my coffee. "I bet that was a hilarious conversation," I grumble.

Jack puts his arm around me and squeezes. "You know I would never laugh at you in front of other people." Fortunately, this is true. He may tease the living daylights out of me, but he protects me like a papa bear when others are around. I lean my head on his shoulder. "Thanks."

We finish our cinnamon rolls and coffee in silence. "Well," I say while bundling my trash together in the takeout bag. "That's that. No more dating for Izzy."

Jack grabs my hand and stops my nervous movements. "You've got to be kidding me Iz. That hunk of a man called me

21

this morning worried about you! You've got to give him another chance."

I shake my head. "No way, José." I jump from my bed and head to the shower.

After a lazy shower, I walk into my bedroom dressed only in a towel to find Jack reading on my bed. "Shit," I yell with my hand on my heart, "you scared me." I walk to the dresser and pull out some underwear. "What are you still doing here?"

Jack doesn't even look up from his reading. "Did you forget lunch with Grandma?"

Face plant. Shit, er, shoot. I did forget. Now I can't spend the day wallowing in my pajamas and eating ice cream. I sigh and turn to my closet for a Grandma-appropriate dress. We are taking Grandma to her favorite restaurant and she has strict dress code standards. I glimpse at Jack and notice he's in the requisite khakis and button-down oxford shirt.

Thirty minutes later we're in Jack's car on our way to pick-up Grandma. I normally don't take long to get ready, but my hair takes forever to dry and Grandma does not approve of wet hair or a sloppy bun. Don't even get her started on pony-tails. You won't survive it! Trust me. Of course, she's right, but mostly I'm too busy to care about the appropriate hair care for the middle-aged.

Grandma is sitting on her porch swing when we arrive. Her front door is locked, she's got her purse in her hands, and her coat is on. Shoot! We must be late. I don't bother to check the clock. I immediately start with the apologies.

"Sorry we're late Grandma," I say as I jump out of the car and walk to the porch to help her. "I had a bad date last night and didn't want to get out of bed this morning." No sense beating around the bush. If Grandma doesn't coerce the truth out of me, Jack will spill the beans anyway.

Grandma doesn't say anything until we're seated in Jack's car on our way to the restaurant. "What did you do now young lady?"

I don't bother pretending I don't know what she's talking about. If her voice, filled with disappointment, doesn't work on me, she'll use her cane. Seriously, you don't want to mess with my grandma. While I'm trying to figure out a way to respond, which doesn't cause any more embarrassment than necessary, Jack fills her in. "Turns out our Izzy mooned an entire restaurant during her date last night."

Jack chuckles, but not Grandma, no Grandma guffaws. When she finally calms down, which feels like it takes freaking forever, she asks, "How did you manage to do that, child? Did you forget to wear knickers?"

"I was wearing a thong," I mumble. I've long been of the opinion that Grandma has selective hearing because somehow she manages to hear the word thong despite her oft issued lament that she is deaf.

"A thong," she chortles. "Don't you know better than to wear dental floss for underwear?"

Jack's driving becomes erratic as he snort laughs. I tune the two of them out for the remainder of the drive. I really don't need to hear the opinions of a gay man and an old lady on what is fashionable underwear for a young lady. Not that I'm a young lady, but you get my meaning.

Despite the somewhat uncomfortable start, lunch with Grandma is always great fun. She drops the subject of my awful date when we reach the restaurant. She has an opinion about everyone and everything – and they're not what you would expect at all! When she's sees a tatted up man enter the pristine restaurant, she sighs and wishes she were 40 years younger. She's not afraid to yell at children who are running around the restaurant acting like little hooligans either. I have to actually keep her from using her cane to deliberately trip young kids, although it's impossible to stop her yelling at the parents for raising hellions. I totally agree with her and can't wait until I'm old enough to spit out my opinions and everyone is too afraid to respond to me.

After we finish lunch and dessert, because it's not a meal out without dessert, Grandma demands we take the long way home and naturally Jack not only agrees but also has no problem assenting to driving way over the speed limit. It's clear where Ryan got his need for speed from. After a not-so-leisurely drive, we drop Grandma off at her house and then Jack takes me home. I'm exhausted and ready for a nap by the time we arrive. Jack grabs my hand before I can escape. "Just. Call.

23

Him." I shake my head and he releases my hand with a groan of frustration.

Chapter 7

"Lightening Crashes" by Live

The phone ringing pulls me out of the zone. Despite my obsession with the most embarrassing date ever and my compulsive need to mull things over in my mind until I think my head will explode, I've managed to get into the zone with my work. I am kicking graphic design butt today! Or at least I was until the phone starts ringing and pulls me out of the zone. I consider not answering, but I'm a bit compulsive about always answering the phone. I mean you never know, right?

"Hello!"

"Izzy? Izzy, is that you?" A desperate voice asks.

"Yeah, it's Izzy. Who's this?"

"It's Ally. I think there's something wrong with Anna. She's not responding." I jump up and start running to the door. Besides being a member of her knitting posse, Ally is also grandma's neighbor and checks in on her a few times a week. This isn't good. "Call 911! Now! I'm on my way."

Grandma's house is only a fifteen minute drive from mine, but by the time I arrive, the police are there as is an ambulance. Shit! I park my car and start running for the house screaming, "Grandma!"

Ally rushes out of the house and runs toward me. She grabs me in a hug. For an old lady, she's pretty strong. Her hug stops me in my tracks. "What's going on, Ally? Where's Grandma?" Only after I ask do I notice the tears streaming down her face. "Ally?" She only shakes her head.

"Oh God," I mutter and release her. I head to the house, but I'm stopped by a cop before I can enter.

"Sorry ma'am. I'm going to have to ask you to wait outside." I look at him as if he's batshit crazy, and then I decide that maybe it's me that's batshit crazy because there's no way in hell he's keeping me out.

"Get out of my way!" I yell. "That is my grandma's house!"

He holds me back. "Is there maybe someone I can call for you?"

I nod. "Yeah, your supervisor because I'm not putting up with your crap!"

Ally is right behind me now and pulling on my arm trying to get me to retreat. "Come on Izzy. You can't help her now."

"I want to see her!" I scream in the cop's face. To his credit, he doesn't back down. He looks at Ally. "Is there someone we can call to calm her down?"

I tune them out and try once again to get into the house, but now both Ally and the cop are holding me back. I'm pretty sure I can kick Ally's ass. She is 70 years old after all, but the cop is built like a ton of bricks, and I'm not moving him an inch. Crap!

I'm staring the cop down when I hear my name being called. "Izzy?" Oh great. And I thought this day couldn't get any worse. I hang my head and turn around.

"What's up?" I ask as if I'm not trying to push a cop out of my way while wearing pajama bottoms, an old t-shirt without a bra, and fuzzy bathroom slippers.

Noel smiles and looks like he's trying not to laugh at the absurdity of the situation. I narrow my eyes at him, and he raises his hands in surrender. "Can I help?"

"Yes," I nod furiously. "I need to get inside to see my grandma and this oaf won't let me pass." I thumb my finger to indicate the cop.

Noel looks at the cop who just shakes his head. I'm pretty sure they've communicated in some weird macho man way, but I don't speak macho man and have no idea what's going on. Noel walks over and pulls me into his arms. "I'm sorry sweetheart," he murmurs into my hair, "but she's gone."

"NO! She can't be gone. She's my only family," I grab onto Noel's shirt and shake him. "She can't be gone," I repeat before my world goes black.

When I wake up, I have no idea where I am until I see my humongous television screen in front of me. How did I get to my apartment? I sit up quickly and shake my head to clear it. I'm fuzzy and disorientated; confused as to why I'm napping on my sofa in the middle of the day.

"Iz," a soft voice beckons beside me. I look to my left and notice Jack sitting on the opposite end of the sofa.

"What? How?" Apparently along with my memory of how I ended up on my sofa in the middle of the day, I've lost my ability to speak.

"Noel brought you home and called me."

Noel? Shit! My memory comes crashing back, unwanted but unstoppable. Grandma's gone. I hiccup as the tears start to fall down my face. Jack rushes to me and folds me in his arms before sitting back on the sofa and cradling me.

"Shhhhh," he murmurs. "It's going to be alright. Everything is going to be alright."

"Alright?" I ask, incredulous. "How is anything ever going to be alright again? I have no one left." I'm crying and gasping. I don't know if Jack can even hear me, let alone understand, until he answers.

"Of course you do. You have me. You'll always have me."

Chapter 8

"Tears in Heaven" by Eric Clapton

I've been in hell for a week by the time Grandma's funeral rolls around. Fortunately, my BFF Jack put his life on hold for the week to help me. I've eaten enough ice cream to fill the Gulf of Mexico and Jack's done his best to finish off a mountain of caramel corn. Let's not even talk about the amount of red wine we've polished off.

I'm staring at myself in the mirror when Jack strolls in. He puts his arms around me and hugs me tightly. He's wearing his black, funeral suit. The same one he bought for Ryan's funeral and hasn't worn since.

"It'll get better," he whispers into my hair. "You know it'll get better. Just get through today."

I nod before turning around and hugging him back. I don't know what I'd do without him. The doorbell rings and I nearly take out Jack's jaw with how quick my head snaps up. "Relax," Jack says. "It's just Noel."

Noel? What the hell is Noel doing here? Jack doesn't give me time to come to grips with Noel's appearance. He merely grabs my hand and pulls me to the front door. Noel stands at the door with a bundle of white lilies, Grandma's favorite. He hands the flowers to Jack and pulls me in for a hug.

"I'm so sorry, baby," he whispers as he holds me tight. I can't wrap my head around why Noel is here let alone why he's hugging me and calling me baby. Nevertheless, I take comfort in his large frame holding me, protecting me until Jack clears his throat and tells us it's time to go.

I start to walk towards Jack's car, but Noel pulls me towards his. "We're going to Grandma's funeral in a GTO?" I stutter.

Jack jumps in place and claps his hands. "Grandma would have liked this car," he says and smiles at me. I smile back, thinking of Grandma and her love of all things übermasculine and totally not old lady like, muscle cars, tattoos, Harleys. Grandma loved them all.

I smile back at Jack. "Grandma would have fucking loved this car." Yes, I'm swearing and I don't care. Sometimes you just need to drop an F-bomb.

We arrive at the funeral home early, but there's already a small crowd gathered at the entrance. Grandma was loved by everyone who knew her. I'm not surprised to see her friends and fellow church goers here to honor her life.

I'm extremely fortunate Grandma planned her death in precise detail. She never talked to me about what she wanted for a funeral or remembrance, but she did tell me who to contact upon her death. The only 'business' I've had to attend to this week is calling her lawyer to get the ball rolling. I'm beyond thankful to her for taking away the need for me to make decisions in my time of grief.

Grandma had apparently requested a 'simple' coffee and cake reception after the service. I don't know how many old ladies you know, but Grandma's friends weren't going to go along with her wish for 'simple' coffee and cake. They've commandeered the VFW hall next to the funeral home and set out a buffet to beat all buffets for after the service. Those women could probably plan a war better than the U.S. government.

I take a deep breath and grab Jack's hand. He pulls me quickly through the crowd into the funeral parlor to our place of honor in the front. Jack and Noel surround me during the service. Jack keeps his arm tight around my shoulders and Noel holds my hand. I try not to cry, but when Grandma's casket is rolled away for the last time, I can't help but let my head fall and the tears flow. Somehow I end up in Noel's arms blubbering away. I don't know how long I cry for but when the tears finally end, he gently grasps my chin and raises my head before kissing my eyes. He smiles tenderly at me, which nearly starts the tears off again.

Jack must sense how fragile and still close to tears I am, because he interrupts by grabbing my hand away from Noel and pulling me toward the exit. I hear Noel's grunt of irritation behind us, but Jack just keeps going.

Grandma wasn't much for standing on ceremony and neither am I. She's thus saved me from having to stand in a receiving line getting condolences from everyone and their mother. I roll my eyes to the ceiling and say a silent thank you to

Grandma's foresight as we leave the funeral home and walk across the street to the VFW.

It may seem strange to hold a funeral lunch at the VFW, but the VFW hall is the center of our community. The hall hosts all important events from Friday fish fries to wedding receptions to bar mitzvahs. You don't need to be a member of the VFW to rent the hall, but Grandma's husband was a veteran and thus it's fitting that her funeral lunch take place here.

"Come on," Jack says to Noel as we enter the hall. "Let's find Iz a place to hang and then get some food. It'll go fast. These ladies can cook!" He actually rubs his hands together in anticipation. I don't know how he manages to maintain his sleek physique with the amount that man puts away.

"I'm fine. I'll be over there." I point to a table in the corner before waving the boys off.

I'm barely seated when Grandma's knitting friends come strolling over. Betty, Ally, Rosemary, Martha, and Rose sit down effectively caging me in. The gang's all here. They collectively lean toward me and motion for me to lean forward as well. What in the world? I look around suspiciously before I comply. I raise my eyebrows in question.

Betty, gang leader that she is, rummages around in her huge purse before finally pulling out a newspaper clipping and handing it to me. It's Grandma's funeral announcement from the local gazette. I don't need to read it. I've already memorized the text. "I don't understand." Why am I whispering?

Betty sighs and points to the article again. I notice a few sentences have been highlighted. *Anna Archer was found dead of natural causes by her neighbor, Mrs. Ally Jackson. Mrs. Archer suffered a massive heart attack while knitting at her home on the morning of…*

After I finish reading the highlighted section, I look up to Betty. "Still not getting it."

Betty huffs at me like I'm a small child who needs to have everything explained to her. "She wouldn't have been knitting. She almost never knitted anymore. She only knitted a bit when we gals got together." Hmm… I hadn't thought about that, but it's true. Grandma didn't knit much anymore. "And besides that, she was complaining about her arthritis on Sunday."

I gasp as I remember the lunch we had with Grandma the Saturday before she died. Grandma had been rubbing her hands more than normal during lunch. I asked her if she was okay, but she had just shrugged and looked away. A telltale sign that the pain was worse than normal.

I shake my head to clear my thoughts. "What are you trying to say?"

Betty leans in even further and whispers. "We think someone killed her."

"Killed her?" I nearly shout, and the ladies quickly shush me. "Who would kill Grandma?"

They shrug their shoulders as one. "We don't know, but something's fishy."

"Are you sure you just haven't been watching too much *Matlock*?" The ladies quickly become indignant, but lucky for me, Jack and Noel arrive at that moment to distract the ladies from their wild accusations of murder. I mean, geesh, everyone loved Grandma. Why would anyone murder her?

The ladies look Jack and Noel up and down like they are pieces of candy. I laugh when I see Noel noticeably gulp, but Jack is eating up the attention – as usual. The ladies quickly, well as quickly as elderly ladies can, stand and move on.

Noel yelps as he sits down. "That lady just pinched my butt," he whispers in horror to me. I pretend to analyze such butt and shrug. "Well, it is a pretty nice butt." Noel starts stuffing his face, but he can't hide the blush that spreads over his face and neck.

Chapter 9

"Listen" by Beyoncé

I'm not given the chance to think about the weird accusations Grandma's knitting group made at the funeral. It's noon, the day after the funeral, and I've had to turn off my phone to try and get some work done. It makes my skin itch, not having the phone on, but the ladies have been bombarding me with phone calls all morning.

Jack returned to his house last night, and I'm trying to get my groove back on with work. Unfortunately, life goes on even without Grandma in it and bills need to be paid. I haven't yet managed an hour of staring at my computer before the front door bell rings. I huff in annoyance, but secretly I'm glad to be off the hook from work for a while.

When I open the front door, Betty pushes her way in without so much as a how do you do. She walks straight to my kitchen table where she puts down a Tupperware cake taker. "Well," she says as she sits down, "are you going to stand at the door all day with your mouth gaping open, or are you going to shut the door and make some coffee?"

Obviously, I've seen the cake and I'm making some coffee. I shut the door and walk to the kitchen to grab coffee mugs and plates. Betty has taken the cake, ooh looks like German chocolate, out of its carrier and pulled a cake knife out of her purse by the time I return to the table with the coffee and plates.

After she dishes up a huge piece of cake for me, which makes her my current all-time favorite person, she leans back in her chair and watches me. I know she wants something. Chocolate cake is, after all, the perfect tool for bribing a forty-year-old woman. But I'm not biting. Well, I am biting – into the cake. I'll hear what she has to say when I'm done.

I debate having a second piece, but Betty is having none of that. She shuts the cake carrier and places it out of my reach. She puts the knife on top of her empty plate but holds onto the handle. I raise my eyebrows at her.

"So," she begins. "Have you had a chance to think about what we said at the funeral?"

I moan and collapse a little in my chair. I don't want to think about Grandma's death and I certainly don't want to entertain the idea she was murdered. Besides the fact that it's utterly preposterous, it's also a little disturbing – okay a lot disturbing.

Betty won't be giving up that easily, however. "You need to do something about it."

"Me?" I squeak. "Why me? You ladies are the ones convinced she was murdered. Why don't you go to the police?"

Betty grunts. "Seriously? Do you think the police will give old ladies two seconds of their time? They'll claim we've been watching too much *Matlock* and kick us out of the station so fast it'll make our heads spin. Just like you did yesterday and are doing now."

My face heats as Betty's arrow hits its target, but I'm not giving in that easy. "Why would someone want to kill Grandma anyway?"

Betty shrugs. "Don't know. The police will need to figure that out." Yeah right. I don't think the police will take me any more seriously than they would Betty and her posse of knitters.

I convince Betty to give me a second helping of German chocolate cake before she leaves. She makes me promise to go to the police before she'll cut me another slice. I don't really promise. It doesn't count if I keep my fingers crossed behind my back and don't actually say the words, "I promise", but just nod when she asks if I promise, right?

I get nearly two hours of work done before the next old lady comes a-calling. This time it's Ally at the door. She hasn't brought any baked goodies to convince me to do her bidding, but I let her in anyway.

We sit on the sofa in the living room and I watch Ally as she wrings her hands. I can't stand it anymore. I have to put her out of her misery – even if it only brings me grief. "What's wrong, Ally?"

She stops her hands and sighs. "Betty told me to come. She said I had to convince you, that I have to tell you what I saw that day."

I gasp. Did Ally see someone? Was Grandma really murdered?

Ally seems to sense my thoughts and shakes her head. "No, it's nothing like that." She takes a deep breath. "It's not like I saw something unusual or anything, but Betty says it's important."

Betty is obviously the head instigator and troublemaker in this tale. I harrumph. Not like I'm surprised or anything. I shake my head and get back to the discussion at hand. "Okay. Tell me what you saw."

Ally takes a deep breath before beginning, "Well, you know I always checked up on Anna on Tuesday mornings." When she pauses, I nod to encourage her to continue. "Normally, she was puttering around the house, but she didn't answer the door so I knocked again and then walked in." She turns to me. "I normally wouldn't just walk in. I promise. But I waited and her car was in the drive. I was worried she had fallen or something."

I grab Ally's hand and smile at her. "I know Ally. It's not a big deal. It's not like Grandma would have minded you walking into her house anyway."

Ally holds my hand tighter as she continues her story. "I was shocked to see Anna sitting in her recliner with her feet up. She never sat in the recliner during the day, only at night when she was watching her shows." She pauses to gather her thoughts before carrying on. "Her knitting basket was next to her and it was a mess. It looked like someone had been pawing through it. And her knitting was on her lap, but it wasn't like she had been knitting. It was more like someone had thrown some knitting on her lap."

"What do you mean?" I ask, my curiosity piqued.

"Well, the needles were just laying on top of her hands. She wasn't holding on to them. And there was no yarn pulled out. The ball of yarn was just lying next to her needles." She starts to talk quickly now. "And it wasn't even the piece she was working on last time the group met. This was something she hadn't worked on for a while. A delicate piece her hands could no longer handle."

I know which delicate piece Ally means, and it nearly breaks my heart to think of it. When Ryan and I first married, Grandma was super excited about the prospect of great-grandchildren. She started to knit some onesies for us. It didn't take me long to figure out that I didn't want children with Ryan though, at least not right away. He was still a child himself. I didn't think I could handle having two children to raise. Grandma was undeterred and kept bugging me and continued knitting onesies until her arthritic hands couldn't take it anymore. The last onesie she was working on was always in her basket though. It was nearly finished, but she couldn't work on it anymore.

I can't listen to any more of Ally's story. I can't handle any more information. The wound is still raw. Luckily, Ally understands. She stands before leaning over to give me a kiss on the cheek and a pat on the head. I'm still sitting on the sofa when I hear the door shut.

Chapter 10

"Call the Police" by James Morrison

I toss and turn most of the night, unable to sleep due to Ally's revelations and my kinda sorta promise to Betty to go to the police. I'm sure the police will think I'm crazy if I claim my eighty-something-year-old Grandma was murdered when she obviously died of a heart attack. I hit the pillow hard in frustration. Screw it! Maybe I should just go to the police. If they don't believe me, then my duty is done, and I can get on with my life. Decision made, I finally fall asleep.

Of course, I'm feeling less confident when morning arrives, convinced the police will indeed think I'm coo-coo for cocoa puffs. I've made up my mind, however, and I'm nothing if not stubborn. And okay, to be perfectly honest, I also don't look forward to dealing with Betty and her crew if I don't go to the police. Those ladies are tenacious as hell!

I arrive alone at the police station shortly after nine. Jack wanted to come with me. He insisted even though I feel bad for taking him away from his life for a week. Turns out he had a rare work emergency and had to back out at the last minute anyway. I catch my reflection in the glass door as I walk in. When I see my tight jeans and t-shirt, I almost turn around. I definitely should have thought about my wardrobe selection before leaving the house this morning. I start to think up a gazillion reasons to chicken out, but stop myself. What if Grandma really was killed?

But how to approach the situation? Do I just go up to the desk sergeant and say "'Someone killed my grandma, do something about it!'"? Unfortunately, standing here thinking about how to handle things isn't going to get me home any faster. I force myself to march up to the desk and nearly shout, "I need to report a crime."

The bored desk sergeant only looks up from her magazine for two seconds before returning to it. "Have a seat."

I don't move. "Aren't you going to at least call someone?"

The desk sergeant, who obviously finds her job extremely tiring, raises her head to stare at me. "I said have a seat." She then uses a shocking pink nail to point at a row of chairs against the wall.

"Fine," I huff and move to sit down. Some people have obviously chosen the wrong career.

It takes about two hours for someone to finally come out from the bowels of the police station to help me. Or ten minutes according to the clock on the wall, but I'm pretty sure the clock is rigged. I follow the man to his desk and take a seat.

The police officer starts up his computer before turning to me. "How can we help?"

Time for the police to think I've gone batty. "I think my grandma was murdered."

To his credit, the cop merely blinks a few times in surprise before he starts asking questions. "And why do you think that?"

Here comes the crazy part. "Well, she was found with knitting needles in her lap, but she doesn't knit anymore."

The cop clears his voice loudly before continuing. "Okay. Let's start over. Who is your grandma? How and when did she die?"

I quickly explain that my grandma is Anna Archer and she died a week ago.

"How did she die?"

"She had a heart attack."

"So," the cop struggles to continue, "you think someone faked her having a heart attack."

Yes! He gets it. I bob my head up and down. "Exactly!"

"And why would anyone kill your grandma? Was she rich? Who would benefit from her death?"

"Um...," I stall for time because I don't have any clue what the answers to his questions are. Actually, that's not entirely true. "I think Grandma had some money. I don't know how much, but she didn't have any living relatives so she made a trust for charity."

The cop narrows his eyes at me. "She didn't have any relatives, but you call her Grandma?"

My face burns. "She's my late husband's grandmother." The cop nods in understanding. One benefit of being a widow? People tend to let things slide when you mention your dead husband. A situation I've had to take advantage of in the past. Not that I'm proud of it or anything, but when needs must...

"Listen," the cop rolls his chair closer to me as he begins, "I'm not sure there's really a crime here."

I don't let him continue. This is bullshit! Sometime between listening to the knitting crew's murder hypothesis and my trip to the police station, I realized that something is indeed not right with Grandma's death. Maybe I don't entirely believe she was killed, but something isn't right. You know that little voice inside your head? The one that tells you not to walk down dark alleys late at night? My little voice was shouting at me that something was up.

I stand up and jerk away. "Fine! I'll figure it out myself." I may have shouted a teensy bit. I begin walking toward the front desk and the exit of the building, but I'm stopped by someone shouting my name.

"Izzy? What are you doing here?" Oh crap, just when I thought my discomfort can't get any worse. Bam! The universe proves me wrong.

I could try to ignore Noel, but that doesn't seem prudent when he's a detective, and I'm in the police station. I turn around slowly and put on a plastic smile. "Hi Noel!" Even to me my voice sounds fake.

Noel grabs my hand and pulls me into an interrogation room. Or at least I assume it's an interrogation room since the sparse decoration only includes one scarred table, four chairs, and a mirror, which covers one entire wall. Oh yeah, and the sign on the door that says interrogation room #2 probably gave it away as well.

Once we're in the room, Noel turns and shuts the door. He jumps right in. "Why have you been ignoring my calls, Izzy?"

I hang my head. Seriously, is it that hard to figure out? The man is a detective, after all. Shouldn't he have a clue? I clear my throat. "Noel, you're nice and all, but seriously, were you not at the restaurant when I mooned the entire dining area? You are way out of my league."

Noel shakes his head. "Isn't that my decision?"

I sigh and look up at him. "I don't want to embarrass you every time we're in public. You deserve better."

I don't know if Noel didn't hear me or decides to ignore me. Probably the latter. "Why are you here anyway?"

Is it possible for my face to get any redder? I think not. "We think grandma was murdered," I mumble to the floor.

Noel grabs my chin and forces me to look at him. "Why don't I take you out to dinner tonight and you can explain it all to me?"

I want to say no. This man is only going to break my heart when he realizes that I am indeed out of his league, but I've got to figure out what happened to Grandma, and it looks like the police are going to be of no help. I straighten my back with determination. I will go out with Noel. I'll probably suffer heartbreak, but that's nothing new. Been there. Done that. Have the t-shirt to prove it.

Chapter 11

"With a Little Help from my Friends" by Joe Cocker

I have no idea what to wear on my 'date' with Noel. I mean, yeah, it *is* a date. But, on the other hand, I'm only going because I want him to help me with Grandma's murder or whatever it is. Face plant. I'm a complete jerk-a-lerk. I can't only go out with Noel because I want to use him. I grab my phone and hit Noel's number to cancel the date, but, of course, the one time I call him, he doesn't pick up. Grrrr…

I settle on something between hot date clothes and work meeting outfit. This translates into work pants with a flirty blouse. Not too shabby, if I do say so myself. "What in the world?" Great, Jack's here.

I turn and look at him. "What?" I don't wait for a reply but go back to applying make-up.

"What are you wearing?"

"Um, clothes." Seriously, is this the dumbest conversation ever?

"I thought you had a date with Noel."

I put down my mascara wand and place my hands on my hips. "And how do you know I have a date with Noel?"

Jack shrugs, but he doesn't look chagrined. "Noel told me."

"What? Are you two buddies now?"

Jack puts his hands in his jeans pockets and shrugs again, but doesn't say anything. I cross my arms on my chest and plant my feet shoulder width apart. Jack knows perfectly well this translates to *answer me or else.*

"Fine," Jack puts his hands up in surrender. "Yes, we're friends."

"Freaking great," I mutter. "That's not gonna be awkward at all when things don't work out."

Jack sighs and reaches forward to pull me in his arms. "Why do you assume things won't work out?"

"Seriously Jack," I complain. "He's so far out of my league I'm surprised the dating police haven't hauled him away for a grievous felony."

"Oh, good Lord woman! When did you lose your confidence in yourself?" Jack spins me around to face the mirror. "Look at yourself. You're pretty. You have a great career. You're hilarious and fun to be with. What's not to love?"

"You're forgetting clumsy, lacks brain-to-mouth filter, and embarrassing." Jack only snorts in response. I decide to enlighten him further. "Number one," I use my fingers to count off my violations. "He met me while I was not-so-gracefully shooting tequila. After which, I proceeded to scream at my speed date, nearly fall over my chair, and then run out of the bar like the devil was on my heels. That's two. Let's not forget number three during which I mooned an *entire* restaurant on our first date. And, finally, today, aka number four, I screamed at a police officer while at the station."

Jack reaches forward and runs his knuckles down my face. "And yet he's still calling you, stood by you at Grandma's funeral, and is excited to be going out on a date with you."

"Excited?" That can't be right, but Jack nods. "Really?" I need double assurance on this one. Jack nods again. "I'm nervous," I admit.

"About what? You're never nervous." That's not exactly true, I'm just really good at hiding my nerves behind snarky comments. Jack should know this by now.

"I haven't, you know... been with a man since Ryan," I admit and feel my face burn with the humiliation of it all.

"But Ryan's been dead five years!" Jack yells, but then stills. "Oh, okay." Now he feels me. He pulls me in for a hug. "It'll be alright. When things get that far, just tell Noel. Any man who can't understand, isn't worth your time."

I nod. Jack is done being Mr. Sensitive and pulls away. "So," he claps his hands in excitement, "now that's all settled, what are you gonna wear?" He cocks a hip and points his finger up and down my body. "Because that outfit, ain't doing it for anybody."

By the time I've applied my make-up, Jack has gathered all of my 'date' clothes onto the bed for his perusal. I may agree that Noel kinda sorta wants to actually see me and maybe, just maybe, is only slightly out of my league, but there's no way I'm changing into date clothes. Why tempt fate?

I plant my hands on my hips and face Jack. "Nuh uh, not gonna happen." I point to the clothes and shake my head.

Jack groans and mumbles, "Why me?" under his breath, but loud enough to make sure I can hear him. He grabs a pair of skinny jeans and shoves them at me. "At least change those hideous pants."

"Fine," I huff and quickly get out of my work pants and shimmy into the skinny jeans. When I've changed, Jack hands me a pair of heels so high that I'll probably get a nosebleed if I wear them. Yeah right, like that's gonna happen. I just shake my head at him. After much bickering, we finally agree that I can wear flats as long as they are sparkly.

I'm just stepping into my sparkly no-heeled sandals, when the doorbell rings. Jack claps his hands in excitement. "Your beau is here," he says before running to the front door. Whose date was this anyway?

Chapter 12

"Walking on Sunshine" by Katrina and the Waves

Needing a little Dutch courage for this conversation with Noel, I'm on my second glass of wine when he finally gets around to asking about my trip to the police station. "Why, exactly, do you think your grandma was murdered?" His question is blunt, but he looks sincere.

"Well," I start, and put down my wine glass to avoid any spillage should my hands start talking on my behalf. "It just doesn't add up." Noel cocks an eyebrow in question. "There are a few things. First, she never sits in her recliner during the day. Like Never. But that's where she was found. She was also found with knitting on her lap, but she doesn't knit anymore because of her arthritis. Well, she knits at the knitting group but not really. Oh yeah, and the knitting wasn't really knitting."

Noel shakes his head in confusion. "The knitting wasn't really knitting?"

I bob my head in confirmation. "Yeah, it was just knitting stuff laying on her lap, but not like you would have if you were knitting. There was no yarn attached to the piece she was working on. Oh, that's another thing," I'm starting to talk faster and faster in my excitement. "The knitting piece was a delicate piece that she hadn't worked on in years." I gulp to calm myself as I think of the onesie. Noel reaches across the table and grabs my hand, silently giving me support. "She couldn't work on it, you see, it was too difficult with her hands. She had really bad arthritis and was having a bad bout of it over the weekend as well." I take a deep breath and lean back in my chair. Confident that I've convinced Noel something's afoot.

Noel lets go of my hand and leans back as well. "I admit this all seems strange, but why do you think it's murder?"

I shrug. "I'm not really sure of anything, but you know that little voice in the back of your head?" He nods in agreement. "It's screaming at me that something's not right."

Noel is quiet for a few minutes. I'm tempted to say something as I'm not good with quiet. I like to fill silence with ramblings about inane and inappropriate stuff. Finally, Noel replies. "Okay, let's just assume that, despite the evidence to the contrary, your grandma was killed." He puts one hand up in the stop position before I can object. "Why would someone want to kill her?"

I slump in my chair. This is indeed the crux of the problem. "I don't know. Everyone loved her."

"So you've basically got two problems. One, she died of a heart attack."

I can't let that go. "But aren't there ways to fake a heart attack?"

Noel nods. "There are, but they are sophisticated methods. Which brings me to problem number two: Where's the motive? Who wanted to kill her? And why?"

As much as it pains me to admit, Noel's right. In order for there to be a murder, there has to be a murderer. And who in the world could that be? Our food arrives and we drop the discussion of grandma's death for the time being, but I'm not going to let it go that easy. This is my grandma we're talking about. She was my rock when I needed one. I owe it to her to find out what happened. If anything unusual happened, that is.

I'm drinking my third glass of wine when I catch sight of Ed, speed dating disaster number one. I nearly drop my glass as I duck my head so he doesn't see me. Of course, Noel the detective, notices. I'm starting to see why old girlfriends had a problem with dating a detective. It's one thing to notice every little nuance, but can't he pretend sometimes not to see everything?

Noel leans over and mock whispers, "What's wrong?"

"It's one of my dates from the speed dating," I answer as I try to hide my head with my hair.

Noel looks around curiously. "Where?"

"Over there," I mutter under my breath and point my head toward the bar where Ed is sitting.

Noel checks Ed out and then asks, "Which one was this?" On our first date, I had told Noel all about my three speed dating disasters. Noel is smiling, obviously amused by my discomfort. I glare at him, but he's staring at Ed.

"The guy who was into BDSM." I try to talk without moving my lips, terrified Ed is going to notice me.

"What? I can't understand you."

I groan. "The guy who's into BDSM." Oops, that came out a bit loud. I think the entire restaurant has stopped talking to stare at me. My cheeks flush, and I stare at the floor wondering if I can hide under the table or if an escape is worth a try.

Noel, however, isn't bothered at all. This is evidenced when he leans back and starts to laugh – loudly. I glare at him, but he continues to laugh until the restaurant goes back to normal. I dare to peek at Ed, but he somehow hasn't noticed the commotion in the restaurant from his perch in the bar. Pheew.

Noel is still laughing and it's starting to annoy me. I cross my arms across my chest and lean forward. "I told you I was out of your league and embarrassing to boot!"

He slowly stops laughing and wipes tears from his eyes. "Babe, you are precious. I think it's me that's out of your league. Every time I'm with you it's an adventure."

"An adventure," I huff. "Watching me embarrass myself is an adventure?" I'm no longer annoyed, now I'm getting mad.

Noel's face turns serious. He leans forward. "You're the only one who thinks you're embarrassing. The other diners barely noticed you. Well, the men are checking you out, but that's a different matter."

Men, checking me out? Nah. Oh wait, he's just trying to distract me. Before I can reply, Noel continues, "When I'm with you, I feel alive. I never know what's going to come out of that delectable mouth of yours. It feels like every second with you is an adventure. No one's ever made me feel that way before." Well, shit. Now I feel bad for ignoring his calls.

"Really?" I sound breathless and feel like a teenage girl with her first crush.

"Really. Now, let's find a desert to 'share', which I only get a spoonful of before you confiscate it." He's smiling at me as if he really believes what he's saying. Huh.

Chapter 13

"I Fought the Law" by The Clash

Motive, motive, motive... the word circles in my mind all night long. If Grandma was murdered, then there has to be a reason why. It's not like faking a heart attack is some bizarre accident or anything. This was planned. Why? Why would someone want to hurt grandma, let alone murder her? I listen to the thunderstorm outside my window and try to figure out what to do.

I sit up straight in my bed when the idea hits me. I have keys to Grandma's house. I can just go over there and snoop around. There are probably clues the police missed because they were blinded by the fact that grandma was old and appeared to have had a heart attack. Hah! Great idea. I nestle back down into my bed for some much-needed sleep.

The storm breaks and the sun peeking out from the clouds heralds dawn's arrival. I'm up and at 'em early. I want to get to Grandma's house before the world is fully awake. I need to get some work done after all the interruptions from the past few weeks. Okay, that's just an excuse. Truth is – I don't want Ally catching me going in and out of Grandma's house. At least until I have a better idea of whether or not foul play was involved, I don't want the knitting crew constantly checking up on my progress. Betty would probably try to commandeer any and all attempts to solve Grandma's supposed murder. I love Betty and all, but I'm not so good at taking orders even if they do come from a sweet, old lady.

I park my car a block away from Grandma's house. Unfortunately, the grass is wet and muddy from last night's thunderstorm and I'm forced to stroll through the neighborhood instead of sneaking through the woods out back of her house. Since the house sits on a few acres of land, the neighbors aren't super close, but close enough if one of the residents is a peeping tom.

I use my key to enter the front door. After I shut the door behind me, I take a moment to catch my breath. I don't think I've ever been in the house without Grandma being around before. The emptiness catches me by surprise. There's no smell of baking in the oven, no laughter from the knitting group on the porch, and worst of all, no sweet old lady shouting hello as I walk in.

I force myself to get moving after a few moments of silence. I have no idea what I'm looking for. Grandma always kept her house clean and tidy. I notice a bunch of mail lying unopened on her kitchen table. I grab it and stuff it in my bag for perusal later at home. I'm trying to think of places Grandma might have kept to herself. Places that could hide secrets that would lead to murder. I nearly chuckle at this assumption. Grandma, secrets? Yeah, right. That woman was an open book.

The stairs creak as I tip-toe upstairs to have a peek in her bedroom. It seems as good a place as any to keep secret stuff hidden. I'm opening her jewelry case when I hear it – sirens. My heart stops. Are the police coming for me? I shake my head and nearly laugh at the ridiculousness of it. Of course the police aren't coming for me.

Just to make sure, I pull back the curtain in the bedroom while standing hidden to the side. Shit! There's a police car in the driveway! Uh oh! Without thinking, I spin around and run down the stairs and out the back door. I head for the copse of woods at the rear of the land.

"Police! Stop!" I hear someone yell, but there's no way I'm stopping now.

"Police! Stop!" The second time the words are shouted, I turn around to see how far the voice is behind me. A large, burly cop is chasing me, and it looks like he's catching up as well. Oh bugger! I sprint for the woods, but I hit a patch of mud and start sliding. Oh no, I'm going down. I land on my butt in the mud – hard. I scramble to get up as quickly as possible, covering myself head to toe in mud, but the burly cop is upon me.

"Just stay down," he yells at me and turns me so I'm face down in the mud. Apparently, I was in need of a mud facial. He slaps cuffs on me faster than you can say howdy-doody and roughly hauls me to my feet. "Come on, missy, it's off to the station with you." He grabs my bag from where it's fallen next to me and drags me to his squad car.

The officer looks my mud-covered body up and down before pushing me up against the car and ordering me to stay.

He pulls a towel from the trunk and places it on the back seat before forcing me into the car. The towel smells like dog piss. How lovely.

We arrive at the police station in full glory – sirens blazing and lights flashing. I don't know why the cop is in such a hurry. I know I'm not. He parks his vehicle behind the station before opening the rear door to grab me. I don't see the purpose in protesting and keep my mouth shut for once. When he realizes I'm not going to make a run for it, his grasp on my arm eases. He pulls me through the station to a desk where he sits me down on a chair while he takes his spot behind a battered ancient computer.

"Now," he begins, "can you tell me what you were doing?"

I shrug and open my mouth to respond when I hear a shout. "Iz?" Oh shit, seriously? Two days in a row? What are the chances? I try to slide down in my chair and hide myself, but it's a bit tricky with handcuffs on.

"Izzy?" The voice is closer now, right in front of me, in fact. I keep my head low but peek up to see Noel staring at me with his mouth wide open. "What in the world?"

I shrug. "I went to Grandma's to find motive," I mumble.

Noel tilts his head back and laughs. He bends over, holding his stomach. After a few minutes of this not-humiliating-at-all moment, he wipes his eyes and grabs his keychain. "I got this," he tells the officer who brought me in before he reaches around and unlocks my handcuffs.

When I'm free, he grabs my purse with one hand and my elbow with another before dragging me back to 'our' spot – interrogation room #2. "Sit down," he says and points to the chair. I sit in the chair he indicated, and he places my bag on the table in front of me.

"Explain, please." He's back in cop mode now: arms crossed over his chest and feet planted shoulder-width apart.

Another shrug. "Not much to explain. I let myself into Grandma's house to search for clues." Noel snorts, but otherwise doesn't respond. "The police came and I ran."

"Why did you run? And how come you're covered in mud?"

"I don't know why I ran." I shrug yet again. "Instinct I guess. You see a cop coming after you and you run." Now is probably not the moment to regale Noel with tales of my wild youth and dalliances with police as a juvenile. "Maybe not the smartest thing to do was run into the backyard, which was a tad bit wet from last night's storm."

"Where's your car?"

"A block from the house."

Noel pulls out his phone and dials. "Hey! I've got your BFF down here at the station. I can't leave. Can you come pick her up?" He nods as he listens to someone on the other end, I assume is Jack. I knew those two being friends was a bad idea. "Make sure you bring towels." Face plant. Jack is never going to let me live this down.

Noel finishes his call, and puts his phone back in his pocket before walking around to kneel in front of me. He grabs my chin and forces me to look at him. "Can you leave the police work to the police?" he asks gently.

I shake my head. "But the police aren't doing anything," I whine. Yes, whine.

His eyes gentle. "You could have been hurt, baby."

I love hearing the words baby come out of his mouth and be directed at me, but I can't stop my pursuit of Grandma's killer. "Nothing would have happened. I had every right to be there. I just panicked when I heard the police sirens."

"Promise me you'll be more careful," He demands and I nod.

Noel has to get back to work. He gets me a coffee and a towel, gives me a quick peck on the cheek, and then leaves me to await Jack's arrival. Jack arrives like the diva he likes to pretend he is. "Where is my Izzy," he shouts as he flounces about. He's got an armful of towels and his camera. The cheek of that man! Noel appears from out of nowhere and Jack shoves the towels at him. Hands free, Jack proceeds to take a gazillion pictures. I'm thinking my five minutes of fame will be on Facebook today.

Chapter 14

"Please Read The Letter" by Robert Plant

I spend the afternoon listening to the never-ending sound of pings from my computer as my Facebook fame grows. I hate Jack right now. Not that I'm surprised, but still, I hate him. I give up on social media and work at dinner time. I shuffle into the kitchen in search of something easy to make. Okay, fine, I admit it, I'm heading for the freezer and my favorite lovers – Ben and Jerry.

When I enter the kitchen, I see my bag sitting on the table. It's filthy and in need of a good wash. I grab it and throw the contents on the table, intent on emptying it before throwing it in the washing machine. Hoorah for canvas bags! Along with a plethora of junk – various lip glosses, nail files, receipts, gum wrappers, etc. – out tumbles Grandma's mail. Huh, in the aftermath of my police arrest and mud bath, I completely forgot about the mail.

I slump into a chair and stare. Should I open it? Now that opening the mail is a possibility, I realize what an invasion of privacy it would be. I'm not sure it's possible to invade the privacy of someone who has passed, but you get what I mean.

I chew on my fingernails while trying to decide what to do. When I'm down to my pinky, I finally decide to open the mail. It's not like this mystery is going to solve itself! I reach forward and grab the pile. First things first, I throw away all the junk mail – of which there is a lot. Marketers must think old ladies are pushovers judging by the amount of sweepstakes Grandma has won.

With the pile much smaller now, I remove everything that looks like a bill. I don't know how many times I told Grandma I could handle her bills online. Didn't matter. She said she liked to balance her checkbook each month. Yeah right. I don't know anyone who *likes* to balance a checkbook.

There are a few larger, colored envelopes and these I pull out and open. I'm not surprised to see several invitations to weddings and baby showers. I think grandma was invited to every wedding, which happened at her church. Probably because she gives such awesome presents. My breath catches

51

in my throat – used to give such awesome presents, I force myself to think.

In the end, there is one extremely official-looking envelope remaining. The envelope itself feels expensive as it's made some from heavy-duty cream paper. The return address is a law office. I clap my hands in glee. Now we're getting somewhere. I only hesitate for a moment before ripping the envelope open.

Dear Mrs. Archer,

As per our meeting and discussion on April 15th, the signed documents have been notarized and filed as per your instructions. Per our standing agreement, our fees have been deducted from the annual retainer. We look forward to continuing to work with you in the future. Please let us know if we can be of any further assistance in this matter.

Yours sincerely,

Huh. None of the letter makes any sense. I read it again, but I'm still confused. After five minutes of staring at the letter, the only thing I've been able to figure out is that it's from the law firm I called to get the ball rolling after Grandma's death.

I pick up the phone and dial Betty's number. "Hello!" Betty answers on the first ring.

"Hi Betty, it's Izzy."

"Oh Izzy, my girl, how are you doing?"

I clear my throat. "Um okay." Gosh, I hope she didn't hear about me being hauled off to jail, but that's a pipe dream. There's no way Ally missed that spectacular show. "I have a question."

Betty doesn't hesitate to reply. "Sure. What is it?"

"I've been going through Grandma's mail, and I found a letter from a lawyer that doesn't make any sense."

"I'll be right over," Betty replies and hangs up before I have a chance to say anything. Shoot. I don't want Betty commandeering this so-called investigation.

The doorbell rings a short time later, but when I open the door it's not Betty standing on the stoop. Or rather it's not only

52

Betty, somehow she has rounded up the troops and gathered them at my house in less than half an hour. Ally, Rosemary, Martha, and Rose stand next to Betty on the other side of my door. This should be interesting. At least Betty is holding a cake carrier and Ally has a pie plate in her hands.

The ladies shuffle in, and sit at my dining room table. I start the coffeemaker while gathering cups, plates, and forks. By the time the coffee is finished and I walk into the dining area, the ladies have dished out pie and cake.

Betty immediately takes over. "So," she starts. "Have a seat Izzy and let's get started." She actually takes out a notebook and pen, then flicks the notebook open and looks at me. "What's happening?"

I grab the letter from my back pocket where I stuffed it when the doorbell rang. "I found this letter from her lawyer in her mail, but it doesn't make any sense."

Ally grabs the letter and hands it to Betty as if they're co-conspirators. Betty reads the letter aloud and then hands it back to me. "First of all," she says while tapping her pen and doing a darn good impression of Jessica Fletcher. "Does anyone know anything about this?"

Four women shake their heads while I shrug. "I'm totally confused. I didn't even know she had attorneys on retainer."

Ally clears her throat and looks to Betty as if to ask permission to speak. Betty nods her head in acquiescence. "Well, yes, I knew that." I gasp and Ally blushes. "Sorry, Izzy, but someone had to drive Anna to the lawyer, and she said she didn't want to bother you." She shrugs, but continues to blush. "I thought she told you."

I'm pretty sure I'm doing an awesome imitation of a gaping fish at the moment. "What," I sputter.

"Now, now," Betty says. "Let's not get our panties in a twist. Anna was allowed to have her secrets."

Secrets! Why would she have secrets from me? Betty doesn't give me a chance to respond. "The question is," she continues, "what was this letter about? And does it have anything to do with her murder?"

Ally shrugs. "I never went into the offices with her, and she never talked to me about it."

Betty looks around the table. "Anyone else Anna confided in?" Betty looks at each woman in turn, and waits until each shakes her head in the negative before proceeding to the next woman. When she has finished non-verbally questioning the table, she turns her gaze to me. She shuts her notebook and clasps her hands on top of it. "There's only one option then. You'll need to call the law office and find out what this is about."

"Me?" I sputter. "But I'm not her real grand-daughter, you know!"

"Sorry, but you're the closest thing to a relative Anna had. You'll have the best luck."

After that announcement, Betty dives into her piece of pie, which apparently signals to the other ladies the discussion is over and it's time for refreshments. The group leaves shortly thereafter, but not before Betty makes me promise to call the law office first thing in the morning. She actually makes me use the words 'I promise' this time.

I'm not sure when law firms open, so I wait until half past nine just to make sure. My hands tremble as I dial the number. "Jones, Smith, and Cagney law office. How may I direct your call?"

"Um. I'd like to speak to Mr. Smith, please."

"May I ask who's calling?"

"This is Izzy Archer."

"Hold on a sec."

A minute later a man's voice comes on the line. "Mrs. Archer?"

"Yes, this is Izzy Archer."

Before I can start my spiel, Mr. Smith continues. "I'm so sorry I haven't been in touch yet. I've been meaning to call and set up an appointment."

I'm too confused to find words in response. He was expecting my call? He wants to set up an appointment? What? I hear papers shuffle. "Would tomorrow morning at ten suit you?"

I manage to mumble yes and the appointment is set.

Chapter 15

"Dream Weaver" by Gary Wright

I'm extremely nervous about the meeting with the lawyer. What if I'm just barking up the wrong tree? Grandma was in her late eighties. Why can't I accept that she died of a heart attack? By the time it's late enough for me to drive to the meeting, I've been prowling around my house for two hours. I leave early from my house and end up arriving fifteen minutes early for my appointment. I stare at the chairs in the waiting room, but I'm too full of nervous energy to sit, so I start pacing the area. After five minutes and about two gazillion meaningful stares from the receptionist, I give in and sit down, although my knees don't get the message and continue to bounce.

"Mrs. Archer," I hear someone call my name and see an older lady with her gray hair tied in a perfect chignon standing next to the receptionist's desk. I stand, and she motions for me to follow her. After a short trek through the hallway, we arrive at a door. She knocks but doesn't wait for a response before entering.

A surprisingly handsome young man stands from behind his desk. "I'm Mr. Smith. Mrs. Archer, I presume?" I nod. "Please have a seat," he says as he motions toward a table and chairs in the corner of his office.

"Can I get you anything?" perfect chignon lady asks.

"Um, coffee?" She nods in response and retreats, closing the door in her wake.

Mr. Smith ushers me to the table, and I sit. He doesn't speak at first, arranging his files. I can't handle the silence any longer and blurt out, "You're awfully young." Ugh! I really need to go to Walmart and see if they sell brain-to-mouth filters.

Mr. Smith smiles at me. "Don't worry. I'm perfectly qualified."

I shake my head. "Sorry. It's just that I can't see my grandma using such a young lawyer." But then I take a second look at him and change my mind. He is a fine specimen of the male creature. Blond, wavy hair a tad long for a lawyer, and sparkling bright, blue eyes – although that could be because he's laughing at me. His suit is pulled taut over his shoulders and biceps. He's hiding a fit body underneath that boring, conservative suit. I casually scratch my nose to ensure there's no drool escaping my mouth.

"Well, actually," he says and finally stops shuffling paperwork. "My father normally handles your grandmother's legal issues, but he's semi-retired now."

I nearly jump out of my seat when a cup of coffee is placed before me. Chignon lady is apparently a ninja in training, I didn't hear the door open or her walking over. I place my hand over my heart and try to breathe normally. My anxiousness about this meeting is skyrocketing by the second. I need to calm down. I should have asked for tea or maybe valium. Yeah, valium would have been good.

"So," Mr. Smith says as he takes a drink of his coffee that has magically appeared before him. "Should we get started?"

I nod and pull the letter out of my purse. "Yes, this is the letter I called you about." I hand it to him and wait as he reads it.

"Actually, Mrs. Archer," he starts, but I interrupt him. "Please, call me Izzy." I don't like being referred to as a Mrs. as if I'm dependent on a man and not independent. I nearly snort. As if my man was ever dependable for anything but a good time.

"Oh," Mr. Jones' voice brings me back to the present. "This letter was written by my father. I actually called you in for a different reason."

"Then you don't know anything about this letter?" How disappointing. "But wait. Why am I here then?" Oops. Said that aloud.

Mr. Jones points to the papers on the table. "The reading of Mrs. Archer's will, of course."

Of course. There's no of course here. Why would I need to be present for Grandma's will reading? "But that has nothing to do with me."

Mr. Jones smiles, but it's condescending. Or is that pity? Either way, not a good look on him. "But it does Mrs. Archer, er, Izzy."

I leave the law firm an hour later in a complete daze. I can't believe what just happened. I shake my head. I must be dreaming. I'm probably still in my bed tossing and turning and this meeting hasn't even happened yet. Yep! That must be it. Except, my dreams are never this vivid. I'm always blind in my dreams, unable to open my eyes. I widen my eyes and look around. Huh, everything seems to be normal, although I do feel like someone is watching me. I shiver as I feel someone's eyes boring into me.

Feeling weirded out, I decide to walk across the street to the diner. I can never find a bathroom in my dreams. If I can find a restroom and actually use it, then maybe I'm not dreaming.

The bell rings as I stroll in. The waitress looks up and smiles. "Can I use your restroom?"

"Sure, honey," she says and points down the hallway. "On your right."

I walk down the hallway and find the restroom. Continuing to test my dream theory, I use the facilities. Huh. This is crazy. This is the most vivid dream of my life. I find a booth and sit down. I still feel eyes following my every move. Man, this is one spooky dream. The waitress strolls over with a menu, but I waive it away. Since this must be a dream, I might as well live it up.

"Waffles with chocolate ice cream and whipped cream, please."

"Anything to drink?"

Perhaps it's a good thing this place doesn't serve liquor because getting drunk before noon seems incredibly appealing at the moment. Only because I'm dreaming, I would never drink alcohol with breakfast otherwise. And if you believe that, I have some prime real estate in the swampland for sale as well.

The waffles arrive quickly, and I woof them down. For a dream, these waffles are delicious! My phone rings just as I finish licking the plate. "Hello," I answer cheerfully.

"You sound happy, babe," Noel responds.

"I'm having the best dream ever!"

Noel chuckles. "Dream?"

58

"Duh, this has to be a dream."

"Why's that?"

"Cuz this can't be real. So it has to be a dream. Duh." Dream Noel is a bit slow.

"Izzy, where are you?" He sounds concerned. Uh oh, is this where the dream becomes a nightmare?

"I'm at the diner across the street from Grandma's lawyer." Shouldn't he know where I am? In my dreams, the players always know everything. Then again, I've never had a 'normal' about Noel before. He hangs up without responding. That's weird, but then again, this a dream.

I'm strolling out the diner when Noel runs up to me. He grabs my head and studies my face. I scrunch my nose at him. "What's up with you?"

"What's going on Izzy? Why do you think you're dreaming?" He sounds out of breath. Now that's more like my dream Noel.

I shrug. "Because it can't be true."

"What can't be true?"

"It can't be true that Grandma was a millionaire and left me everything."

Noel's eyes widen in surprise and then he pulls me to him and hugs me tight. "Izzy, this isn't a dream?"

"Not a dream? Of course, it's a dream."

Noel pulls away and shakes me slightly. "Izzy, please, it's not a dream. You're awake."

"I'm awake?" I ask just before the curtain comes down.

Chapter 16

"Price Tag" by Jesse J

I awake cradled in Noel's arms on my couch. I snuggle into him. I don't remember how I got here, but I'm no fool – I'm taking advantage. I hear someone clear their throat and snuggle even closer to Noel. I'm not ready to be interrupted.

"Iz," a very irritated Jack says. "Now is not the time."

"Why not?" I pout. Noel laughs, kisses my forehead, and then gently lifts me off his lap and places me next to him on the couch. I snarl at Jack, but he's immune to my snarls. Bummer.

"What's going on?" I ask when the silence lasts more than two seconds. That's two seconds too long in my non-stop talking book.

Noel grabs my hand. "You thought you were dreaming."

I snort. "Well, of course I was dreaming. And now I'm awake." Seems simple to me really.

Jack grabs my purse and starts digging around. "Hey! What are you doing?" He pulls out a bundle of paper and flips through it. "Shit, Iz," he says and hands the bundle to Noel.

Noel raises his eyebrows and hands the papers to me. He doesn't even take a peek! Gotta love that guy. Well, not love, love, but you know what I mean. I look down at the bundle and it all comes back to me. I gasp. "Damn. It wasn't a dream."

Noel puts his arm around me and squeezes. "No, it wasn't a dream, baby."

I drop my head. "I knew it felt too real to be a dream, and now I'm going to have to run five hundred million gazillion miles to work off the waffles and ice cream for breakfast."

Jack laughs and shakes his head. "Seriously, Iz? You just became a millionaire, and you're worried about what you had for breakfast." I roll my eyes at him. "Where did she get all this money?" he asks.

I shrug. "I asked, but baby Mr. Jones didn't know much about it. He said I'd have to ask Daddy Jones. That reminds me,"

I dig through the papers until I find the letter, which started my trek to the lawyer's office and hand it to Noel. "Looking for clues."

He doesn't look at the letter. "Izzy," he says calmly. "The fact that your grandma was a millionaire and kept it a secret is a clue."

I shrug. "If no one knew, they wouldn't kill her for the money, now would they?"

He shakes his head. "It's impossible no one knew. Someone knew. Someone always knows."

"Okaaay," I say, but I still don't believe him. I mean, if I didn't know she was a millionaire, no one else would either, right? Well, maybe her husband but he died ages ago before I was even on the scene. "But it's not a motive if no one would gain from her death, right?"

Noel smiles. "Yes, whoever would profit from her death has the best motive to murder her," he explains.

I sigh. "So that doesn't help at all since I'm the one who profits from her death."

Noel grabs the papers from my hands and raises an eyebrow at me. "May I?" I nod. He shuffles through the papers quickly and then hands them back. "It looks like you're not the only one who inherits."

That's true. While I thought Grandma had left all her money to charity, it turns out she left the bulk to me and made some small contributions to local charities. They're not actually small contributions, but in comparison to the millions in her bank account they look small. Now I know why she never wanted me to do her finances. Liked to balance her checkbook, my ass!

"I don't think any of the charities she donated to would actually kill her." I roll my eyes to emphasize the ridiculousness of Noel's statement.

"Which charities did she donate to?" Jack asks as he grabs a pen and paper from my purse. I growl at him digging around in my purse again, but he ignores me.

"The church, of course. The VFW, the animal shelter, and the women's shelter," I answer as Jack scribbles notes on the paper. "All worthy causes. I really can't believe anyone from those charities would kill her to get more money out of her. It doesn't make any sense. Grandma gave them money every year anyway. Everyone knew you only had to ask her for a donation and she'd give one." Jack rips a piece of paper from the notepad and hands it to me. He's written each charity down under a large title 'To Check Out'. In case I missed his meaning, he's underlined the title three times.

"Huh," Noel grunts. "Maybe it wasn't someone wanting charity but someone angry she wouldn't give to their cause?"

I shake my head, but Jack speaks before I get a chance. "I can't believe that. She gave money to everyone. She gave beggars on the street money. Anyone who asked for money got it. And I don't think anyone knew she had this much money."

"Well, if you two are convinced no one killed her for her money, and no one killed her for not giving them money, who killed her? If anyone killed her, that is," Noel mutters the last part but I hear him and give him the evil eye, which only makes him smile.

"Don't you believe me that someone killed Grandma?" I don't give him a chance to answer and turn to Jack. "What do you think?"

Jack shrugs. "I find it hard to believe anyone would kill Grandma. I mean she was a firecracker, but she was also the sweetest, kindest person I ever met. She accepted me and never batted an eyelash over the fact that I'm gay." He raises his hands in defense when he sees I'm about to blow up on him. "But, I find it hard to believe that she was sitting in her armchair in the middle of the day with *that* piece on her lap. She obviously wasn't knitting."

Noel clears his throat. "What's the deal with the piece of knitting she had on her lap? Everyone keeps mentioning it as if it has some special meaning."

I sigh and look at Jack, who smiles in encouragement. "Well, when I first married Ryan, Grandma was super excited about having little ones running around. She started knitting these adorable onesies for any children we would have."

"But you don't have any children," Noel interrupts to say.

I nod. "Yeah, I quickly learned my husband was a child himself and was never going to grow up. I worked full-time while he farted around doing pretty much nothing. How was I supposed to have a child with a man who couldn't change the toilet paper roll when it ran out?"

"So you wanted children then?"

I shrug. "Sure, I guess, but it doesn't matter anyway. I'm too old now and Ryan's dead." I clear my throat. "Anyway, after Ryan died, Grandma put the onesie she had been working on in the bottom of her knitting basket. She promised me she wouldn't touch it again out of respect to Ryan. She thought I was still in love with him," I snort.

Noel grabs my hand. "And this was the knitting on her lap when she was found?" Jack and I nod in unison. "And that's why you think she was murdered?" We nod again.

After my bizarre meeting with the lawyer, this melancholic mood is too much for me. I clear my throat and grab the letter from Papa lawyer Smith and hand it to Noel. "That's why we need to find out what this letter is all about."

Noel quickly reads the letter. "This doesn't say much of anything."

"I know. That's why I made an appointment with the real Mr. Smith for the day after tomorrow."

"Okay," Noel says and leans forward to kiss my forehead. "But be careful."

"Careful's my middle name." Noel smiles, but Jack snorts.

Chapter 17

"I Knew You were Trouble" by Taylor Swift

Even Noel admits Grandma's wealth could be a motive for murder. The fact that her wealth was a secret makes the motive possibility that much stronger. Even so, Noel's still not convinced it's murder, which makes the police utterly useless. No big surprise there. It's up to me, I guess.

I have no idea how to investigate a murder or solve a crime of any sort, for that matter. Maybe Google will help. I search 'how to solve a murder' and there are, gulp, over fifty-five million responses, but are any of them useful? Besides my favorite article, which is 'A fifteen-step explanation with pictures included', there isn't anything else that can be of any use. I don't need to know how to set-up a murder mystery evening or win a murder mystery event, for that matter. I don't have time to buy and read a forensic handbook. And I'm certainly not trolling through the FBI's most wanted pictures to help them solve their crimes.

I go back to the fifteen-step illustrated explanation. Only now that I actually read the article instead of looking at the drawings - an occupational hazard - I see there are seventeen steps. First step – find a mystery – is done. Check. Second step – grab some friends – also done. Check. I've also managed to detect secrets and delve into danger. Oh wait! It says to **not** delve into danger. Oops! There's also a rule about tomfoolery. Does taking a mud bath in Grandma's backyard while running from the police count as tomfoolery? Apparently, we're also supposed to wear disguises and be sneaky. That I can do.

What am I doing? Goofing around while reading inane articles on the web isn't going to solve anything. I don't know what I was thinking. I'm a graphic designer. We're not exactly known for following how-ever-many-steps plans or logical thinking in any way for that matter. Of course, I do know someone who can help. Do I dare call Noel to pick his brain on how to solve crimes? We're friends, right? This is what friends do, isn't it? Help each other. Before I can change my mind, I shoot off a text to Noel asking him if he wants to have dinner at my house tonight.

Noel's response *I'd love to baby* makes me feel a teensy-weensy bit guilty. But I've never been one to let guilt stand in my way.

My mother, when we still talked about such things, convinced me I needed a *signature* dish. What's a signature dish? It's a meal that you can make to utter perfection. My dish is lasagna with garlic bread and Caesar salad. Lasagna may be time-consuming, but you can make it in advance and the prep work done before your guests arrive. It's important to have time for a proper cocktail and not be slaving away in the kitchen when you invite people over for dinner.

I go all out with setting the ambiance for the date. I pull out my checkered table cloth, fancy dinnerware, and crystal wine goblets as well as a good bottle of red wine. I've always got lots of the cheap stuff available, but I save the really good bottles for special occasions. Huh. I guess my guilt is bothering me after all.

Noel calls at six to tell me he's running late. He just needs to grab a shower, and he'll be right over. I'm too nervous to sit still, and thinking about Noel naked and wet in a shower doesn't help calm anything down. I grab my laptop and start scrolling through the hits on my earlier Google search, but it really is useless. I thought you could learn anything from the net. Guess not.

The doorbell rings, and I rush to answer it. Wow! Noel is looking absolutely divine in an oxford shirt and dark blue jeans. His hair is wet, and his face is flushed. He prowls toward me and grabs my hips before leaning in and giving me a hard, closed-mouth kiss.

"Wow," I say when he lets me up for air. Shoot! I didn't mean to say that out loud.

Noel chuckles and reaches back to shut the door as he enters. "I'm glad you called, Izzy." Darn it. He's going to make me feel guilty right off the bat.

"Yeah?" I say.

He nods. "Yep. I really like you. It's nice that you like me too and want to spend time with me."

Oh crap. This is not going as planned at all. I decide to ignore his comment as there's no response I can give that won't make me feel like a total jerk. "Come on. Dinner's ready," I say and usher him into the dining room. He sits while I go to the kitchen to grab the lasagna.

"This looks great, Iz," Noel says as he scoops a large portion of lasagna for himself. He piles his plate high with lasagna, bread, and salad.

"So," I ask once we've eaten our first helping, and Noel is on to seconds. "How did you train to become a detective?"

"Police Academy," Noel says in between bites.

"Is that where you learned to solve a murder?"

He raises an eyebrow at me, but answers, "A bit." He shrugs. "Most of it you learn on the job."

"So there's not like a manual or something about how to solve a crime?" I may be pushing it a tiny bit.

Noel sets his fork down to give me his undivided attention. "What's this about Izzy?"

I feel my face heating, but venture forth. "Just curious how the police would go about solving Grandma's murder. If they were going to do anything about it, that is." I'm definitely pushing it now.

"Did you invite me over here for this?" Noel's voice is steel.

I duck my head. "Not entirely," I mumble.

He stands and heads for the front door. "Noel," I call. "That's not the only reason I asked you over, honest."

He turns around and stares at me. His face is granite. "I don't know if I can believe that right now." He stalks toward the door.

I jump up and run to him before he can leave. I grab his arm and pull with all my might, which doesn't move him, but at least he stops. "I do like you. I like you a lot. I like you more than I should, and it scares the hell out of me," I take a breath before continuing, "but I'm also way freaked out about Grandma. I have no idea what's going on. She was a millionaire, and I didn't know. She left everything to me but never told me. What else didn't she tell me? What was going on?"

I drop his arm and walk back to the kitchen table, head drooping. I collapse on a chair with my head on the table. After a few minutes, I feel a warm hand grab my shoulder and squeeze. "I know it's tough losing a loved one, Izzy, but you can't go around thinking it's murder just because your grandma had some secrets."

I nod. "It just doesn't make any sense. She wouldn't be knitting, so why was there yarn and needles on her lap? And why was she in her chair in the middle of the day?"

Noel crouches down next to me and moves my face so I have no choice but to look at him. "Izzy, how do you know it was the middle of the day? When was the last time anyone saw her? When was the last time anyone talked to her?"

And that is why I totally suck at investing anything. I should have thought of that from the very beginning. Maybe the ladies and I are just making something out of nothing. But no, Grandma would never have had the onesie on her lap. Of that, I'm sure. Or am I? I thought I knew Grandma through and through, but I was wrong. Maybe I didn't know the first thing about her.

Noel grabs my hand and tugs me to the living room. He sits me down and then heads to the kitchen. He comes back with the Ben & Jerry's still in the carton and one spoon. The man's a freaking genius, I tell you. He puts in a romantic comedy and watches the entire movie without complaining once about it being a chick flick. When it finishes, he kisses me lightly and leaves.

Crap! This gorgeous detective is giving me every reason to fall in love in with him. I know I should protect my heart from that delectable man, who is so far out of my league, I should be getting nosebleeds when I look at him, but I blame my hormones for being magnetically drawn to him. I'm in trouble.

Chapter 18

"Land of Confusion" by Genesis

Another day, another lawyer's appointment.

When I open the door to the law firm, I run smack dab into a man. "Sorry," I automatically say before looking up. I gasp. It's not often you see a younger man with white hair, but that's not what has me startled. It's the eyes – so dark that they're nearly black. They look like pure evil but strangely familiar. He's staring at me as if I killed his dog. Geesh, I only accidentally ran into him. I shiver and quickly move past him.

The receptionist recognizes me when I walk forward. I'm sure it's because she appreciates my fashion style, and not because I paced the reception area like a caged animal last time.

Perfectly coiffured lady comes to greet me within a minute of my arrival and shows me to an office down the corridor from young Mr. Smith's office. When she opens the door, I nearly gasp in surprise. Old Mr. Smith is not what I expected – at all. Instead of the gray-haired, mass of wrinkled old man I expected, before me stands a very distinguished looking older gentleman. It's clear why grandma was using the Smiths for all her legal needs. I hope they actually know what they're doing and weren't only functioning as eye candy for Grandma.

Mr. Smith smiles and extends a hand. "Ms. Archer I presume." Distinguished gentleman and politically correct? Grandma's knitting group would eat him alive.

After I shake his hand, we move to sit at a large conference table. Coffee cups and a large pot of what I presume is coffee are already set out on the table. Mr. Smith lays down a file and then proceeds to pour me coffee before taking his place opposite me. "My condolences on the loss of your grandmother."

I nod. "Thank you."

"Now," he says as he opens the file in front of him. "My son informed me of why you're here." I sit up straight, listening intently now. I can't wait to hear what's going on. He pulls out a large drawing and unfolds it on the table.

"I have no idea what I'm looking at," I say without thinking.

Mr. Smith smiles and nods at me. "This, Ms. Archer, is your land."

"My what?" I know grandma left me her house and there is a decent sized yard attached, but I wouldn't call it land. At least not in the way Mr. Smith is implying.

"Your land," he repeats. He points to the outline of a house. "This is, er was, Mrs. Archer's house and the surrounding area that belongs to it."

I stand and peer at the drawing, which I now realize is a map of Grandma's house and surroundings. At the bottom, there is a row of houses I recognize as the street she lived on. The rest of the map is basically empty with only lines and numbers scribbled on it, but I have no idea what any of it means. I know that behind Grandma's house and all of the houses on her street, for that matter, are fields and some small copses of woods. The land has lain fallow ever since I can remember. I always assumed each homeowner owned a few acres behind their house.

Mr. Smith points to the area behind the houses and draws an outline with his finger. "All this is your land. There're about fifty acres in all."

"Fifty acres!" I gulp. That's a lot of land.

"That's true." Oops! Guess I said that last part out loud.

I sit back down and take a breath. "Okay," I slowly start. "It seems I now own a bunch of land, but what does that have to do with the letter I asked about?"

"Everything." Mr. Smith folds the map back up and pulls out some paperwork. "Your grandmother came to me to protect the land."

"From what?"

"Everything and anything."

Talk about being vague. "What the heck does that mean?"

"Your grandmother was never really specific with me. She just said that she didn't want anyone to exploit the land."

"I have no idea what you're talking about. What did you do for Grandma?"

Mr. Smith sighs and takes a deep breath as if he is explaining something to a child. It's not my fault I'm confused, it's like he's being deliberately obtuse. "I placed a conservation easement on the land."

"What's a conservation easement?" Apparently my purpose today is to be confused and ask dumb questions.

"Basically, it means the rights of the land are divided between the owner, that's you now, and an environmental group."

I shake my head, but it doesn't make anything clearer. "Well, what rights do I have, and what rights does the environmental group have?"

"Oh, you can basically do anything with the land you would normally do: build a house, farm, have livestock, etc., but the environmental group holds an easement on the mineral and water rights."

"The mineral and water rights? But the land is only meadow. What minerals would be there?"

Mr. Smith shakes his head. "I don't know. Your grandmother never discussed any specific issues with me."

I try to sort the new information out in my head, but frankly I'm a bit overwhelmed at the moment. Apparently I'm not only a millionaire, but a landowner as well. Just a week ago I was working despite my grief to make sure I had enough money for the mortgage, and now I never have to work again. But back to the issue at hand. "Who is this environmental group anyway?"

He shuffles through his papers. "Save the Plains."

I have no idea who or what that is. "When did all of this happen?"

"Just a few months ago."

"And you have no idea why Grandma wanted to do this?"

Mr. Smith shakes his head again. He hands me copies of the paperwork, and that's all there is to it. Although I'm technically wiser than when I arrived at the law office, I'm not any closer to finding out what happened to Grandma. As far as I can tell, this has nothing to do with her death, and here I thought I was the next Nancy Drew.

The phone rings as I'm leaving the law firm. "This is not a dream," Jack says in what he thinks is his spooky voice.

"Ha! Ha! You're so funny. NOT!" I'm never going to live down the whole *thought I was dreaming* thing. It's lovely to have someone like Jack in my life to remind me of every failure and blunder I've ever made. Aren't friends awesome?

Jack ignores my response. "I'm on my way to your house now to hear what you learned," he says and then hangs up without waiting for a response. Sometimes it's annoying having a friend who's so successful, he can come around at the drop of a hat.

Chapter 19

"Building a Mystery" by Sarah McLachlan

My driveway is full of cars by the time I make it home. Oh great, looks like the old lady cavalry has arrived. That's what I get for telling Betty about my meeting with the lawyer. That woman can't keep a secret if her life depended upon it. Although at the age of seventy-five, she probably doesn't give a hoot if her life depends on keeping her mouth quiet.

I'm not really in the mood to deal with Betty and her entourage and debate driving on by my house, but Jack has already spotted me from his perch on my stoop. He waves and I'm stuck. No turning back now. I park the car in the street and walk in the front door yelling, "Honey, I'm home!"

The ladies are gathered around Noel at the dining room table. I wonder what Noel's doing here, but my attention is quickly diverted by the baked goodies on the table. Is that a cheesecake? Noel stands and gives me a quick kiss. I look around and notice the gang's all here. The old lady troop consisting of Betty, Ally, Rosemary, Martha, and Rose as well as Jack and Noel. I swallow my sigh and move to sit down, but there's nowhere to go. Jack's standing in the corner and the ladies plus Noel have commandeered my dining room table and chairs.

Noel grabs my wrist and pulls me to sit down on his lap. As he sits, I see his cheeks turn red. "What's wrong? My fat butt too much for you," I quip.

"No," he whispers. "Someone pinched my ass – again."

I hear a giggle and peer around Noel to see Ally. I raise my eyebrows at her. She blushes and looks down at her feet, but I see a smile appear on her face. I can't help it. I burst out laughing.

Betty obviously thinks we've been goofing around too long and clucks her tongue before clapping her hands to get our attention. "So, Izzy," she looks pointedly at me. "What did you learn today?" Before I can respond, she speaks again. "And maybe you can fill us in on the other meeting as well." Five ladies turn to stare at me with their best guilt-inducing looks.

They're all mothers so they've had lots of practice. I squirm in Noel's lap.

I clear my throat before beginning, "I assume you already learned about the reading of the will." I try to give Jack a stern look, but he refuses to meet my eyes.

"Yes, dear, but we'd like to hear it from you." Betty's good. She's got the *I'll make you feel guilty for even thinking bad thoughts* voice down pat. I would have spent my childhood grounded if I were one of her children.

"There's not much to say about the will. It seems Grandma had quite a bit of money, and she left most of it to me." I shrug and act nonchalant.

"How much money?" Rosemary asks.

"Over a million. Maybe more than two," I mumble.

Betty grunts. "So, whoever knew about the money did it?"

I clear my throat. "There are two problems with that. One, no one knew about the money. And two, it's only a motive for the person inheriting the money, which is me and I didn't do it."

"First things first," Betty responds with a wave of her hand. "We all knew about the money."

I nearly jump out of Noel's lap. "You knew about the money?" I screech. Nods all around the table answer me. "All of you?" Again they each nod. "But why didn't I? And where did the money come from?"

Betty takes the lead again. She really should have been a five-star general. "First of all, where the money came from is no mystery. When Anna's husband got out of the military, he got a small stipend for his injury. He invested in some stocks, made a little money, invested the profit, and so on and so forth." She clears her throat before continuing. "I think we all assumed you knew about the money." She looks around the table in question and nods greet her. Huh, seems I'm the odd man out.

My jaw is on the floor by now. I clear my throat. "So that's why you thought Grandma was killed? For her money?"

I hear murmurings of yes. "But wait I minute!" I just realized something. "If you thought she was murdered for her money, then you must think I killed her because I inherited it!" I try to jump off Noel's lap, but he holds me tight.

"Sshhh, Izzy," he murmurs in my ear. "No one thinks you murdered your grandma." I turn to growl at him, but he just kisses my lips. Damn, those delectable lips distract me.

Ally's quiet voice breaks the silence, which descended after my outburst. "I think I know why Anna never told you about the money." I raise my eyebrows at her and she blushes. "I'm not sure of this." I just stare at her, silently begging her to continue. "I think it was because of your husband."

"Ryan?" Now I'm really confused. "But they didn't have anything to do with each other."

"And if Ryan knew about Anna's money? What then?"

I hang my head. I know exactly what Ally is getting at. Not only was Ryan the epitome of lazy, but he truly believed that he deserved to live like a king. No, not deserved, had a right to have everything his little heart ever desired. Ally's right. If Ryan had known about his grandmother's money, Ryan would have pretended to be a loving grandson while declaring her incompetent behind her back. Grandma was no dummy.

Noel squeezes me tight. I close my eyes and lean into him. I can't blame myself for marrying Ryan. I was young and in love. But I do feel stupid for staying married to him after I fell out of love with him. I couldn't just leave him, though. I had made a commitment.

Jack clears his throat and offers me a sad smile. He was there through all the fights and heartache. I can't believe I've had such good luck to find a friend who is not only great fun to be around, but stands behind me – always. "Anyway," Jack says in an obvious attempt to change the subject. "Did anyone else know about Grandma's will?"

Once again, Ally answers. "Anna told me she was giving all her money to charity. No one knew you were going to inherit," she pauses and turns to smile at me. "We're happy for you though." The tension in the room dissipates as the entire senior citizen brigade smile at me.

"Thanks Ally," I whisper back. "That's what she told me as well – that she donated the money to charity. Well, she did donate some money for charity, but the bulk of it, I inherited."

"So," it's Martha's turn to ask questions now it seems. "What was today's meeting about?"

"A bit of a letdown really. Just some information about a conservation easement," I shrug. "Nothing that would have caused someone to murder her."

"What's a conservation easement?" Rose asks as she dishes out cheesecake.

I explain about Grandma's landholdings and what I think an easement is. I'm still not entirely clear about how the whole thing works. "So you see. No reason to murder anyone there."

"Unless," Jack pipes in, "someone didn't know about the conservation easement and thought they could get the land rights from you."

I splutter. "From me? No one knew I was going to inherit, remember?"

Jack nods. "Okay, get the lands rights from whoever inherited. In fact," he says, his excitement growing, "that makes even more sense."

"But you're not making any sense," I point out.

He begins to pace. "Stay with me. If a mineral company or something wanted the land and thought that a charity would inherit, they could buy the land on the cheap from the charity. A charity would be easy to manipulate." He stands still and turns toward the table with a triumphant grin on his face.

Noel clears his throat. "There might be a few problems with that theory," he says cautiously. "First of all, we have no proof anyone wanted the rights to the land. And why would they kill for the rights? Why not ask your grandma? And," Noel turns to me, "no offense, Izzy, but she was old. Why not just wait for her to die?"

Jack leans against the wall, clearly defeated with Noel's rebuff of his theory. Betty, however, is not so easily defeated. "Ladies, did anyone hear Anna talk about a mineral company wanting her land?"

"It could be another type of company as well. Like maybe a mining company," Jack is quick to add.

"Could this have anything to do with that fracking that's all over the news?" asks Rosemary.

"What's fracking?" Martha, Rose, Ally, and Betty want to know. I want to know as well, but I keep my mouth shut as if I already do know what it is. I look stupid enough on accident, no need to look stupid any more than that.

Luckily, Noel does know what fracking is and explains. "It's this new technique designed to recover gas and oil from rock." Sounds simple enough.

"But why do you ask?" I ask Rosemary.

"A few months ago Anna started going on and on about fracking." She shrugs. "I had no idea what she was talking about. I'd seen it on the news, but I didn't really understand what it was."

Noel turns to me. "When did your grandma put the conservation easement on the land?"

"A few months ago. April, I think."

Jack claps his hands in glee. "It's a clue!"

Noel gives him a look. "Don't get too excited Mr. Happy, it could be nothing."

Jack points his finger at Noel. "You're such a downer. Good thing you're hot." I giggle on Noel's lap and he turns to me. "You think that's funny?" He raises an eyebrow at me and then starts to tickle me. I'm extremely ticklish and in no time I'm nearly falling off his lap. Noel stops and pulls me closer so I'm steady on his lap and proceeds to kiss me.

Jack claps his hands. "You guys are sooo cute," his sarcastic voice is nasally and not attractive. "Can we get back to the case now?" Noel snorts at the word case but keeps his mouth shut.

I turn to look at Jack. "You're full of ideas today. What do you think we should do?"

He takes a minute to think before responding, "We need to find out if some mining company had been talking to Grandma."

"Excellent," Betty claps her hands in excitement. Shit. We're in trouble now. "We'll meet tomorrow morning at Anna's house and conduct a search." She actually used the words 'conduct a search'. She must be OD'ing on detective novels.

I roll my eyes. "I can do this on my own. No need for everyone to go." I say this, but I'm really thinking I don't want the entire posse going through grandma's things. It's such an invasion of privacy. Unfortunately, Betty is not to be deterred.

"Many hands make light work," she quips. I don't even try to argue. There's no way I can win anyway. Call me a coward if you will, but old ladies are tough as nails.

We make plans to meet the next morning at Grandma's, and everyone gets up to leave. When I see Rose start to pack up the cheesecake, I give her a look. She smiles in understanding and puts the yumminess in the frig for me. If everyone is going to invade my house every chance they get, then the least they can do is leave the fracking cheesecake. Still no clue what fracking is.

Chapter 20

"I've been Searching" by Chicago

I don't hold much stock with Jack's idea that a mining company killed Grandma. Even though I doubt the ethics of a mining company, murder seems above and beyond a company's *normal* unethical tactics. I can't deny the timing of events though. Grandma was talking about fracking to her friends and soon after, she was having a conservation easement put on her land. Was she worried about the land, in general? Or was there a specific reason for her concern? Either way it looks like I'm going to have to research just what the heck this freaking fracking is all about.

Like Noel said, fracking is a method of recovering gas and oil from rock. It uses high-pressure water to force the rock to release the gas inside. Sounds dangerous to me, but then again, I'm a graphic designer. What the heck do I know about engineering? I couldn't engineer my way out of a wormhole. Okay, so most people couldn't, but you get my drift.

It's clear why grandma was anti-fracking, if she was indeed anti-fracking. We're just making assumptions about coincidences and coming up with a motive for murder. I can't help wondering if we're making a mountain out of molehill. Anyway, this fracking has lots of environmental groups up in arms. To be fair, most environmental groups are up in arms constantly anyway. Still, it seems they may actually have a point in this case. Fracking uses vast amounts of water, potentially puts carcinogens in the groundwater, and causes earth tremors. Causing earth tremors sounds like flirting with disaster to me.

But first things first, we need to find out if Grandma was actually being courted by a mining company. The Ben-Gay battalion is already at grandma's house when I arrive. I admit I'm a bit late, but these ladies get up at the butt-crack of dawn. How am I supposed to compete with that? I'm not part vampire, I need my sleep.

Jack is waiting on the front porch with the women, but Noel backed out of the search. He has to play adult today and go to work. I push my way through the group to the front door as I'm the one with the key. After everyone is inside and gathered in the front room, I speak. "So, how are we going to do this? Divide and conquer?"

"Yes, you take her roll top desk. It probably has the most private stuff, so you'll want to handle that." Betty has obviously been thinking about the search, and I appreciate her candor. "Jack, you can manage the kitchen." Jack nods in response and heads off. "Rosemary and Martha, you check out the living room and the rest of the downstairs. Rose and I will do the bedrooms upstairs, and Ally will handle Anna's bedroom." She looks to me. "I assume you would feel better with Ally doing Anna's bedroom." I nod in agreement. Ally was Grandma's closest confidante as well as neighbor.

Everyone disperses to begin their searches. I head to the roll top desk in the den. It's locked, but I'm a bit embarrassed to admit that I figured out how to jimmy it open ages ago. I never looked in though, too ashamed by my crime to go any further.

I slowly roll the top open and am nearly brought down by the amount of dust suddenly floating in the air. When was the last time Grandma was in here? And who knew she was such a slob? Her house was always immaculate, but it looks like the roll top desk is where she hid her inner slob. Ugh! I can't work under these conditions. I head to the kitchen for some cleaning supplies.

Jack is meticulously going through every cupboard when I arrive. "Just getting some cleaning supplies," I state in warning as I enter the room although I was tempted to pinch his ass, which is sticking out of the corner cupboard. What can I say? He's got a nice ass.

He crawls out the cabinet he's currently searching and turns to me. "Cleaning supplies? You know we're not here to clean, right?" He stands and brushes off his jeans and hands, his face scrunched in displeasure as he stares at imaginary dust. The kitchen grandma did keep immaculate.

I start pulling stuff out of the pantry before I respond. "I know. It's just so dusty. I'm going to be sneezing for weeks."

Jack pulls me into him. "Are you sure that's it? Is all this maybe a bit much?"

I sigh and lean into him. Of course, he's right. He's always right, which is super annoying. I'm avoiding going through Grandma's things because it means that she's really gone. The wound of grief is still fresh, and it feels like I'm pouring salt on it. Jack squeezes me in a hug.

"I know it's hard, but you're going to have to go through her things eventually anyway. Why not get it over with? Like ripping a bandage off."

Jack stayed beside me through my grief and guilt over Ryan's death. He knows how much I like to dwell. He's probably right that I should just get it over with, but I want to wallow in my grief for a while longer. I still have a few pints of Ben & Jerry's in the freezer, after all. Jack lets go of me and pushes me in the direction of the den. Guess he's done being gentle. "Now go."

I huff. "Fine! But I'm still cleaning the dust."

I hear him chuckle as I walk in the den. I spend the morning cleaning out the desk and organizing Grandma's files. I'm not reading anything yet, just sorting everything into piles. I guess I need to start paying the utilities for the house as well. I put those letters in a separate pile to take home with me. There's a big pile of personal correspondence, and I'll take those home as well. There may be friends that don't live nearby who haven't heard of Grandma's passing. I guess I need to inform them as well. Something else to not look forward to.

It's just past noon when I hear the front door slam closed. "Hello! Lunch is here." I hear Noel shout. An unladylike stampede down the stairs is the response to his shout out.

I walk into the kitchen to find the table piled high with pizzas and the ladies scuttling around finding plates and cutlery. Noel sees me and walks over. He immediately pulls me in for a hug. "How are you holding up?" he whispers into my hair. Gotta love a man who does that!

I shrug. "Okay, I guess." I went on autopilot a while ago – not looking at anything in depth, merely sorting, sorting, and some more sorting.

Noel pulls back to look at my face and gauge my honesty. He nods before sitting and pulling me into his lap. He must have a thing for me sitting there, especially since I'm not the lightest gal around. I don't imagine it's comfortable for Noel and try to get up, but he pulls me back down. "I like you here," he whispers into my ear.

"So," Betty's voice pulls me out of my Noel trance. "Has anyone found anything?" The ladies stop the distribution of pizza slices to look at Betty and shake their heads.

Betty locks her gaze on me. "What about you, Izzy?"

I shake my head as well. "Nothing yet." I don't add that I haven't actually gone through any of Grandma's papers yet.

The ladies chatter away as they eat lunch, but I remain quiet, encased in Noel's arms. When lunch is finished, I jump to help the ladies clean up, but they shoo me away. "Go say goodbye to your beau," Martha says as she pushes me out of the kitchen.

I grab Noel's hand and try to lead him to the front door, but he resists. "What's wrong?"

"I have a few hours before I need to be somewhere. Why don't I help?"

"Really?"

Noel grabs both my hands. "Of course." He lifts my hands up and kisses them gently. What is this guy doing? Trying to make me fall in love with him? "Yes," he responds with a smirk. Shit. I guess I said that out loud. I really need to work on engaging my brain before my mouth opens.

We spend the afternoon going through all of Grandma's files. Noel reads the correspondence I can't be bothered with, which is probably the majority of it. I read the private stuff. I've probably read one letter to Noel's five, but I can't help it. Each letter reminds me of Grandma and brings back memories.

An hour after lunch, Betty finds us. "We've finished our search. How are you two doing?"

I look around at the mass of papers on the floor. "Making progress."

Betty grunts but doesn't respond to my statement. "We're heading out."

I stand from my place on the floor and hug Betty. "Thanks for your help."

She nods. "You're welcome. We've gathered most of her clothes to take to charity. We left the fancy dresses for you to have a look at."

"Wow, thanks." I hadn't even thought about that yet.

"Yeah, well, you're going to need the closet space when you move in," she responds. Move in? I haven't thought about that either. There's lots I need to think about, I guess.

Jack leaves with the ladies after making me promise to call him tonight, and Noel and I settle back down on the den floor.

"Huh," I hear Noel grunt after a while has passed. Don't ask me how long, I've been staring at the same letter since everyone left.

"What's up?"

Noel hands me a letter. "It looks like there was a mining company interested in your grandma's land."

I quickly read the letter. It's an offer for the mineral rights on Grandma's land. I nearly choke when I see for how much. Damn! Grandma could have been super-duper rich!

"Do you see the date on the letter?" I look and see the letter was sent in April, which was about the same time Grandma talked to Mr. Smith about the conservation easement.

"Izzy, I have to say something," Noel says it with such sincerity that I look up startled. "Just because this company wanted her land, and she didn't agree with them, doesn't mean she was murdered." I nod and he continues. "The stuff you read in books or see in movies – that's not how it usually works."

I nod as if I agree, but I'm not paying any attention to his words. Instead, I'm thinking: Why didn't she tell me? What other secrets was she keeping?

Chapter 21

"Ice Cream" by Sarah McClachlan

I call Jack the minute I get home. Noel is off on a stake-out and this is the perfect time to talk to Jack without Noel interrupting. Even though Jack, best BFF ever, agrees to come over right away, I'm nearly finished with the pint of Ben & Jerry's when he arrives. He drops down on the sofa and pries the spoon from my hand. I growl at him, but he ignores me and grabs the pint from my other hand.

"What did you do?" I'm not looking at him, but nonetheless, I can feel his eye roll.

I shake my head. Yes, normally I'm the one who causes my own troubles, but this time it's not me. Or is it me? Is it my untrustworthiness that caused Grandma to create the easement? I drop my head in my hands.

"Izzy," Jack's voice is gentle now. He pulls my chin up and forces me to look at him. "What's going on?"

I try to speak, but nothing comes out. Instead, I choke, and the tears start to flow. "It's Grandma," I wail. "She didn't trust me!"

Jack gathers me in his arms and lends me a shoulder to cry on. "There, there," he says and pats my head. "I'm sure that's not true."

I wrench myself from his arms. "But it is true!" I shout. "She put that stupid easement on the land because she thought I would sell out!"

Jack crosses his arms and stares at me. "What are you talking about?"

I wipe furiously at the tears streaming from my eyes. Now I'm getting angry. The sweet Grandma I knew. The one I loved and mourned didn't trust me. It's the ultimate betrayal! I take deep breaths to calm myself before replying, "There was a mining company interested in the land. They offered her millions for the mineral rights. She didn't think I could refuse the money. That's why she put the easement on the land."

Jack puts up his hands. "Hold on. How do you know that's why she put the easement on the land? Did she say anything? Write anything? Tell someone anything?"

"Why else would she do it?" I scream – yes scream – at him.

"Okay, you're going to need to calm down if you want to figure this out."

"Calm down! Don't tell me to fucking calm down! Grandma didn't trust me!" I'm surprised the glass isn't shattering with the shrillness of my screaming now.

Jack leans back and crosses his arms. He knows better than to say anything else to me at the moment. He'll wait me out. Bastard knows I need to let off some steam. I pace around the house for a good fifteen minutes before I finally settle.

Jack smiles at me. "Now," he says and pats the seat next to him on the sofa. He waits until I'm seated before continuing. "What's going on?"

"Noel found a letter from some mining company. They offered Grandma several million dollars for the mineral rights on her land. It was written about the same time she contacted her lawyer about putting the easement on the land."

Noel nods. "Is that all?"

I glare at him, but nod in response.

"And now you think grandma thought you were unreliable and not to be trusted?" I nod again. "Exaggerate much?" My glare intensifies, and I may growl a bit. Jack grabs my hands. "That woman loved you more than her own flesh and blood. She left you millions. How does that translate to untrusting?"

"Maybe you're right." But I'm not willing to give up completely.

"Come on, you know I'm right," Jack says and pushes me.

"Fine." I throw my hands in the air. "You're right." I stick my tongue out at him.

He squeezes my shoulders. "I understand you miss her. Sometimes, you just need to have a meltdown." And now he's done being the supportive friend. "Back to the case. Were there any other letters, threats?"

"You still think it's murder?"

Jack nods. "You have to admit the letter is a fabulous clue."

I shake my head. "Noel disagrees. He says it doesn't prove anything."

Jack grunts. "Sometimes Noel is such a fuddy duddy." I agree, but don't say anything. "I say it's a clue. Now," he claps his hands in excitement, "how should we proceed?"

I shake my head. "I have no idea." I wonder if there is a solving murders for dummies book. Lord knows Google was no help.

"I know," Jack leaps from the sofa in excitement. "You need to go snoop around at the mining company."

"What?" I jump up and stare him down. He's obviously gone loco. "Are you out of your flipping mind? Did you forget that I ended up in the back of cop car for going through my grandma's house? How the heck am I going to snoop around a mining company's offices?" I really don't fancy the idea of going to prison. Who does, for that matter?

Jack deflates. "Huh, you may have a point there." I raise my eyebrows at him. "Okay, okay, you do have a point."

We both collapse back onto the sofa. "Maybe we should call Betty," Jack suggests. I just look at him, but don't deem to respond. "Yeah, you're probably right. There's got to be another angle here. Something we're forgetting."

I close my eyes and lean back into the sofa. I'm physically exhausted from my temper tantrum and mentally drained from going through grandma's house. I don't really want to think about anything anymore, except maybe how I can wrestle the ice cream back from Jack. Unfortunately, Jack's undeterred.

"Let's go over this one more time, and then you can have your precious ice cream back." Jack's a mind reader. I nod.

"Okay, first the mining company contacted Grandma and offered her lots of money for the mineral rights to her land."

"Yep," I say, my eyes still closed.

"Then, Grandma contacts the lawyer to protect the land. He suggests putting an easement on the land." Jack pauses for a moment. "How does this easement work again?"

I shrug. "From what I understand, Grandma gave specific mineral rights – probably those the mining company were after – to a conservation group."

Jack jumps up and claps. "That's it! That's the missing piece. The conservation group."

I open my eyes now. He may be on to something.

"Do you know which group it is?" I nod. "Okay then, call them and meet with them. They may have more information."

"Great idea, Jack!" I jump up and hug him.

"Now can I have my ice cream back?"

Chapter 22

"Contagious" by Avril Lavigne

The conservation group, Save the Plains, is super excited to hear from me. The office manager actually uses the words 'super excited'. They can't wait to meet me, and I make an appointment for the next day. I probably should do some *real* work in the meantime, but it's hard to get motivated to sit behind a computer when you're chasing a murderer – although 'chase' may be a bit of an exaggeration. Oh, and I'm a millionaire now.

I'm surprised by the offices of Save the Plains. They're light and airy. I was expecting an office stuck in someone's basement with boxes crowding the hallways. Everyone is young and overly friendly. It's a bit creepy. I think I prefer a dank basement.

I'm shown into a meeting room where a young woman is waiting my arrival. She stands and nearly runs to me when I enter. "Hi, I'm Jenny Williams." She looks as if she's about to hug me, but I stick out my hand. I'm not into hugging strangers. Jenny looks at my hand and shrugs before shaking it vigorously. Her enthusiasm is nearly catching. Lucky for me, as a middle-aged cynic, I'm immune to such naïve enthusiasm. I manage, just barely, not to roll my eyes at her.

"I'm Izzy Archer," I state and pull my hand away before she breaks bones. Maybe I should have endured the hug?

"Yes," she says and points to a chair for me to sit on, flouncing down on a chair opposite mine. "I've been looking forward to meeting you."

"You have? Why?" My cynic is on high alert.

She actually blushes. I didn't think anyone blushed anymore. "I wanted to thank you for your generous gift."

"Um," I stutter – a bit embarrassed that she's thanking me for something I was screaming about yesterday. "That was my grandmother, not me."

Jenny waves her hands in dismissal. "Doesn't matter who started it. It's your land, right?"

I nod. "Actually," I take a deep breath before starting again, "I wanted to talk to you about the easement."

Jenny takes a quick breath. "You're not thinking of backing out are you? There's no backsies possible."

I laugh at her use of the juvenile term 'backsies' and shake my head. "No, no. I have no problem with the gift in itself. I just wanted some background information."

She visibly releases the breath she was holding. "Oh good. We don't need another heir fighting us. Legal fees are killer." After a pause, she asks, "Anyway, what do you want to know?"

I squirm in my seat a bit, uncomfortable with the questions I want to ask. "To be honest, Grandma didn't tell me about the easement. I'm wondering why she made it. I mean, I know it's to protect the land, but do you know anything about my grandma's situation, in particular?"

Jenny shakes her head. "Actually, I just started in this office. Let me see who handled the easement and if they're available." I nod at her, and she jumps up from her chair.

After five minutes of waiting, during which time I learn, once again, that I suck at mobile phone games, Jenny returns. She sits across from me and shakes her head. "I'm sorry, but the person who handled your grandma's file isn't here today."

"Oh," I say, deflated. "Will they be in anytime soon?"

"She's gone this week, but will be back on Monday."

"Can I see her then?"

Jenny nods. I'm disappointed I have to wait, but at least it's not a complete dead end. Jenny sets up an appointment for me on Monday morning, and within a few minutes I'm back in my car cruising for home.

I get a weird feeling of déjà vu while driving home, almost like someone is following me. I know I'm crazy, but that doesn't stop me from checking my rearview mirrors constantly. I shiver. Can you catch paranoia from overdosing on Ben & Jerry's ice cream?

I shake my head to clear it. I am not going to get all paranoid. What I am going to do is drive home and get back into the swing of things. I've wasted enough time since Grandma's death and even though I'm now a millionaire, I need to get some work done. I haven't had the time or energy to think about my future and whether I'll keep working, but I need to, at least, finish the projects to which I've already committed myself. It looks like Jenny's enthusiasm for life is contagious, after all.

I jump out of my car and walk to my front door with renewed energy. I'm surprised to see my front door wide open. I guess Jack's made an appearance. "Jack, you left the door open!" I yell as I enter the house. No one responds. Huh, that's weird. I nearly jump out of my skin when I hear a roar. I whip my head around and look outside. It's just a car starting up – an awesome Chevy Impala muscle car – but just a car, nonetheless.

I let out the breath I was holding as I watch the car slowly roll by. Just as the car is passing, the driver turns his head and stares at me. His shocking white hair looks familiar, but I can't place it. I shake my head and slam the door shut. *I will not be paranoid. I will not be paranoid.* I say it out loud because everyone knows talking out loud scares away ghosts and creepy things.

I call Jack and fill him in on the meeting. He's disappointed the clue he discovered didn't pan out but excited I'm going to meet with someone else on Monday. He wants to join me then, but I manage to persuade him it would be weird. He pouts, but I don't let him distract me. I've had years of practice in ignoring his pouts.

Chapter 23

"Bleeding Love" by Leona Lewis

My phone ringing wakes me up on Saturday morning. I look at my alarm clock and groan. It's only nine. Who dares to call me this early on a Saturday? Can only be Jack. "What?" That may have come out a bit like Oscar the Grouch, but I always sympathized with poor Oscar. He was totally underappreciated just because he lived in a garbage can. The garbage can looked clean enough to me. Who am I to judge? And he was kind of cute – for a grouch.

I hear chuckling on the line, which definitely doesn't sound like Jack. Face plant into pillow. "I thought you were Jack," I say into the pillow. For some reason, this causes the chuckling to gain tempo. The men in my life are such jerks sometimes. But they're also extremely hot, which means I put up with them. Who wouldn't?

"You're very chipper in the morning," Noel says, after he finally stops laughing.

I sit up in bed and force myself to sound civil. "I stayed up late working last night, trying to catch up on projects." I yawn to emphasize my point.

"Oh," Noel sounds disappointed. "Does that mean you're working all weekend?"

I sigh. "Probably, why?"

"I thought I'd take you out on a date tonight. Just you and me. No Jack." Hmmm... work or date with hot police detective? No contest there.

"Well," I try to play coy. "It's not like I'm going to work 24/7. I guess I could make some time for you."

Flirty Noel makes an appearance. "You could, could you?" I smile but remain quiet. "I'll pick you up at six. See you then, baby."

"Bye." My voice probably sounds breathless, but it does weird things to me when he calls me baby.

I really do need to catch up on some work projects. I spend the day locked away – literally – in my home office. I put the chain on the front door to prevent Jack from wandering in and turn off my phone. Although my mind often wanders to a certain hot piece of male deliciousness, I manage to get quite a bit of work done before my phone alarm goes off at five. I still don't understand how the alarm works when the phone's turned off, but I'm not complaining.

The doorbell rings at five minutes to six. I rush to answer it, but then force myself to slow down before I open the door. "Hi," I say when I see Noel standing there looking scrumptious in dark jeans molded perfectly to his strong thighs and a button-down shirt. He's holding a bunch of vibrantly colored tulips. "Someone is getting insider information," I say as I grab the tulips. I try to turn toward the kitchen, but Noel refuses to release his grasp on the tulips.

"Is that any way to greet your man?" he says as he leans forward and gives me a hard kiss on the mouth.

"That seems like a better greeting," I admit when I can breathe again. This time when I try to turn toward the kitchen with the flowers, he lets me, but not before he smacks me lightly on the butt. "What?" I sputter.

Noel chuckles behind me as he follows me to the kitchen. I quickly sort out the flowers, and we're on our way. We drive in Noel's ultra-hot GTO to a small Italian restaurant in the downtown area. I'm determined I'm not going to ruin this date in any way. There will be no embarrassing myself by flashing my backside to the restaurant, and there most certainly will not be any loud talking of BDSM. I'll even try not to pepper Noel with questions about murder investigations. I will be the perfect date. I barely stop myself from snorting at that thought.

I skip wine and ask for sparkling water. Wine tends to cause my brain to disconnect from my mouth. I scrounge the menu for a meal with the least amount of spillage opportunities. Definitely not ordering anything with spaghetti or cream sauce. I'm not the most elegant eater in the best of circumstances, and when Noel's around I tend to turn into a lovesick teenager. A lovesick teenager may be borderline okay, but a lovesick teenager with sauce dribbling down her chin is a definite no-no. Tortellini it is!

Dinner is really great, if I do say so myself. Of course, I would have had a good time if I could have just stared at Noel for an hour, maybe two. He seems to enjoy my chattering away, though, and I manage not to talk too loudly about embarrassing things. No talk of whips and chains tonight.

"Do you want coffee?" Noel asks after we've finished our scrumptious meal.

"I'd love some."

"How about we get out of here, ,take a stroll, and then grab a coffee at the corner coffee shop?" Noel suggests. Who knew hot guys could be closet romantics? Well, obviously we don't. Otherwise they wouldn't be in the closet, but you get my meaning.

Noel and I stroll around the downtown area hand in hand. I window shop and Noel people watches. After a stop for coffee, we head to his car and he points his car toward my house. I'm getting really nervous. I'm not really sure what to do at this stage. Should I invite Noel in? If I do, how far should I let things go? Ugh, this dating thing isn't easy.

Noel grabs my hand and squeezes. "Relax, Iz. We won't do anything you don't want to do." I chuckle. That's not the problem. I know what I want to do, but I don't know if it's appropriate. Apparently, there's a big difference.

Noel parks in my driveway. "Stay there," he says before getting out. He walks around the car and comes to the passenger side to open my door for me. "My lady," he says as he offers me his hand.

"My, my," I respond in my best English accent. "I do declare you are a gentleman, Mr. Blackburn." He bows slightly before pulling me out of the car.

I walk up to the door fiddling with my keys. Ask Noel in? Not ask Noel in? What to do? I don't know why I'm bothering to pretend it's a struggle. We all know I want Noel to come in with me. I put the key into the lock and turn to ask Noel if he wants to come in, but he doesn't give me a chance to talk. Instead, he grabs my face gently between his hands and leans in. He kisses me until I can't breathe.

"Do you want to come in?" I ask when I finally catch my breath. In response, Noel gently pushes me out of the way and unlocks the door. He grabs my hand and pulls me inside. I turn on the hall light and throw my purse and keys on the little side table I keep in the entrance way for such things because otherwise I would spend half my life trying to find my keys.

When I look up to check my reflection in the mirror above the side table, I let out a little scream. My lower face is covered in blood. I turn to Noel and see he's got blood gushing from his nose. "What the..." are the only words he gets out before he collapses to the floor. Huh. Didn't figure big, bad, hot detective man for a fainter.

I rush to the kitchen and wet a towel before returning to the hallway where I've left Noel laying on the floor. No chance of moving that man. I mop up the blood on his face and use the towel to stem further bleeding before I try to wake him. I slap his shoulder none too gently. "Noel, wake up!" I don't shout, but I'm not exactly quiet either.

His eyes open, but they're unfocused. He's obviously confused. "Where, what?" he says before his eyes clear. "Shit."

"Come on," I say. "Let's try to get you seated." I get behind him and reach under his arms to pull him up. He's limp and weighs a ton. Hard muscles may look delicious, but they sure are heavy! After a bit of unladylike grunting, I manage to get him leaned up against the wall.

"Lean your head back, it'll slow down the bleeding," I have no clue really, but it sounds good. "Are you feeling okay?" Stupid question, I know. "Should we take you to the hospital?"

Noel shakes his head just as the doorbell rings. Who in the world is ringing the doorbell at this time of night? I open the door to find Jack standing there looking irritated. When he sees my face, he lets out a shriek. "What's going on here?" he asks as he pushes me inside.

I ignore him and turn on Noel. "You promised me a night without Jack!" I accuse with my hands on my hips. He shrugs, but I can't hear any response as he's holding the towel in front of his mouth.

"What in the world is going on here?" Jack shouts. Yes, shouts. I don't think I've ever heard Jack shout before. I turn to stare at him. He points to my face and makes a disgusted look. "You've got blood all over you, and Noel is on the ground holding a towel to his nose. What in the world did you do to him, Iz?"

"Me! I didn't do anything. He got a nosebleed and fainted!"

Jack looks back and forth between the two of us in bewilderment before he realizes the truth of what I said. Then, he throws his head back and laughs. "I don't know what's funnier," he manages to say in between chuckles, "the fact that you two were obviously making out when he had a bloody nose or that Noel fainted." Noel growls at the last part.

I ignore Jack's comments. "What are you doing here, Jack?"

He turns to me. "You haven't been answering your phone all day."

Oops! I smack my forehead. "I turned my phone off to get some work done. I must have forgotten to turn it back on. Sorry." I reach over to give him a hug, but he backs away.

"Uh uh," he says as he points to my face. "You need to clean that shit up before you come any closer, Izzy girl."

"Wimp," I say under my breath but deliberately loud enough for Jack to hear. He ignores me and leans down to Noel.

"You okay man?"

Noel nods and stands up. "Yeah, I think I'm good now." He takes the towel away from his face.

"Your face doesn't look much better than hers," Jack comments.

I turn on Jack. "I don't think you're needed here tonight," I tell him and then grab Noel's hand. I drag him to the bathroom where I clean up his face.

"You okay?" I ask. He nods, but he won't look me in the eyes.

We get cleaned up and then Noel hightails it out of my house. It appears the fates are determined I end up alone. I reach for the corkscrew.

Chapter 24

"I Never Knew You" by Jason Mraz

I spend Sunday much the same way as Saturday – locked away in my office. This time I'm not excited about my date with Noel. Instead, I'm thinking he's running as far and as fast away from me as he can. Not too surprising. I didn't expect it would work out anyway. Sighing the day away won't help anything. Doesn't stop me though.

Jack calls to beg me once again to let him join me at my meeting with the conservation group. He really thinks he's some kind of detective or something. *Or something* is about right. I put him off with promises of calling right after my meeting. He pouts but agrees with me – eventually.

Jenny, the overenthusiastic girl I met on my first trip to Save the Plains, is waiting to greet me when I arrive at the offices on Monday morning. "Hi Izzy," she nearly shouts as I walk into the office. Is she bouncing on her toes?

"Jenny," I respond. I start to reach out my hand for a handshake, but then decide against it. She nearly crushed me last time. I smile instead.

"Come on," Jenny says as she turns around. She flounces down the hallway and I follow. I don't flounce.

Jenny shows me into the same conference room we used last week. There is an older woman, who looks vaguely familiar, in the room. She stands as I enter. "You must be Izzy Archer," she says and reaches out to shake my hand. "I'm Delilah. Please have a seat." I grab a chair across from her.

"I'm sorry about your grandmother. She was a great woman."

I nod. "Yes, she was." I stare at her, head tilting to the side in confusion. "Do I know you?"

Delilah smiles. "You may have seen me at your grandmother's funeral."

"Of course. Thank you for coming." The words fall automatically from my mouth.

Delilah clears her throat. "Anyway, you wanted to see me?"

I shake my head to clear it. "Yes. I understand you dealt with my grandmother and the conservation easement." She nods. I take a big breath before continuing. "You see, Grandma never told me about the easement. Well, she never told me I was going to inherit either. But that's another story. Anyway, do you have any idea why she wanted an easement?"

"I do." She begins and then stops, re-considering her words. She clears her voice before starting again. "Actually, I don't know how much I should tell you. If she didn't mention this to you, then..." She trails off and shrugs her shoulders.

I take another deep breath to stop myself from getting annoyed. After all, Delilah is only trying to do the right thing. She can't know we suspect Grandma was killed, and I'm not about to tell her. Or am I? "I understand your reluctance. And I appreciate your loyalty to my grandmother. It's just that we're concerned about some irregularities." There, that sounded pretty detective-like, didn't it?

Delilah's head whips up. "Irregularities? You're not thinking of fighting the easement are you."

I groan. Seriously? Is that the only thing people worry about around here? I shake my head. "No of course not. If that's what my grandmother wanted, then I will honor her wishes. But," now my voice is turning more urgent, "we have concerns about her death." Delilah gasps. "I'm not saying she was murdered or anything, but we need to investigate the possibilities."

Delilah studies me for a minute before she responds. "Well, I guess it wouldn't hurt anything if I gave you a bit of background." I bob my head enthusiastically. She leans back in her chair. "Anna, your grandmother, came to me a few months ago. I guess it was sometime in April. She wanted to know what her options were to protect her land from mining companies."

I nod. "Yes, I saw the letter from Ajax Mining offering Grandma three million dollars for the mining rights on her land."

Delilah smiles in relief. Obviously I'm not completely in the dark. "She told me they sent several letters and that a rep from the company kept calling her and stopping by unannounced to talk to her." I raise my eyebrows in surprise. Grandma wouldn't have liked that one bit! "She told them no, but they kept pestering her, asking her questions about the land, who would inherit, stuff like that."

"Wow," I say. "They were really bothering her."

Delilah nods. "Unfortunately, they were. She thought the easiest way to get rid of them would be to make it legally impossible for them to get the land. She talked to her lawyer and he suggested talking to us about an easement." She shrugs. "And that's basically it."

I try to think of questions a real detective would ask. "Um, was she afraid for her life?"

"No," Delilah shakes her head. "I don't think so. She was always feisty and not scared of anyone or anything. As I'm sure you know."

"And a troublemaker," I add with a smile. I really suck at this detective thing. I can't think of any more questions. "Well," I say as I stand. "Thanks for your time."

"Sure," Delilah says, obviously relieved with my departure. "Anytime." Such a liar. A sweet woman, but a liar, nonetheless. She never wants to see me again.

Jenny is waiting by the door to the conference room. "Did you find out everything you need to know?" She asks as she escorts me to the exit.

"Yep," I say, but don't give her any details. Jenny looks disappointed, but I don't give into her pouty face.

I drive slowly back to my house. My mind is all over the place. It sounds like Ajax Mining was harassing Grandma, but why didn't she tell anyone? It's not like she could protect herself. Once her husband died, she got rid of all the guns in the house. What was she going to do – attack them with a rolling pin? Or maybe her knitting needles?

I park in my driveway and pull out my phone and keys. I need to call Jack before he starts blowing up my phone for information. The front door's open. Guess Jack didn't wait for me to call him back. "Jack?" I yell as I walk in the front door and stop in shock. My house is a freaking mess! "What the...?"

Chapter 25

"I'm a Mess" by Ed Sheeran

I stop and dial Jack. "Izzy! What did you find out?" He's breathless with excitement.

"Be quiet for a second, will you!" I take a breath to calm myself. "Sorry, but my house was broken into."

"What? Where are you? Get out of there! Someone may still be inside." For once in my life, I'm listening to a man. I back out of the house.

"Okay, I'm outside."

"Get in your car and call the police. I'm on my way." Jack hangs up. I call the station and give my location.

I'm still sitting in my car when the police arrive. They tap on my window and I roll it down. "Yes," I say in a small voice, which I'll probably be embarrassed about later.

"What's going on?" the officer asks.

I swallow loudly. "I came home and the front door was open." I shrug. "I sometimes forget to lock it and it blows open. Anyway, I walked in and the house was a mess. It looks like someone destroyed everything."

The officer nods. "Stay here." He proceeds to the house with his partner. After a few minutes, they come out and stand on my stoop talking.

Jack arrives and runs to my car. He pulls me out for a big hug. "Are you okay?"

"I'm fine," I say. The shaking has mostly subsided, but I'm not looking forward to going into the house.

The officers walk up to us. "The house is clear. There's no one here. Can you go inside and see if anything's missing? Try not to touch too much."

I nod and grab Jack's hand. Before we make it into the house, Noel pulls up and runs to me. "Izzy, are you okay? What happened?" He reaches out to hug me, but I squeeze Jack's hand. Jack understands and shields me from him.

"What are you doing here?" I ask before shaking my head. "Never mind. I'm fine. Someone ransacked my house. I'm just gonna have a look to see if anything was taken." Noel gives me a look I can't interpret before he stalks off to talk to the other police officers. I turn and head into the house, dragging Jack behind me.

Jack and I reach the house and he gasps. "Oh my God, Izzy. Thank God you weren't here when this happened." He shivers.

By now I'm numb and only manage to nod in response. "I'll check my office and bedroom. Can you check down here?"

Jack nods absently, but I'm already headed up the stairs. I check my office first. I don't want to see what the maniac did to my bedroom. I gasp when I look in. Everything is gone. My computer, my tablet, my hard drive, everything. Shit. That's gonna cost me.

I move onto my bedroom. It's a disaster area. My clothes are strewn about the room. The sheets and blankets have been torn from my bed, the mattress overturned. The ensuite bathroom doesn't look much better. The entire contents from my vanity have been removed and thrown everywhere. Who would do such a thing?

I walk back downstairs to find Jack and Noel conversing in low tones in the living room. The two police officers are sitting at the table filling out paperwork. I walk up to them. "All of my computer equipment is missing," I tell them. "As well as my financial files."

I don't have many paper files as I keep most things electronically. Jack walks over and hugs me. "Oh Izzy, what are you gonna do?"

I shrug. "It'll be fine. I have an online backup drive. I e-mailed the projects I finished over the weekend this morning so I didn't lose any work."

Jack hugs me tighter but doesn't respond. The police officers start to ask a zillion questions. Do I have any enemies? Are my files worth money? Have I gotten into any fights lately? Blah, blah, blah. I answer their questions truthfully, but I don't mention our investigations into Grandma's murder. Since it's not really a murder – yet – there isn't much to tell and it's not lying to omit something. Also, I'm afraid that they'll think my elevator doesn't go all the way to the top.

After thirty minutes of questions, the officers finally pack up and leave. I notice Noel doesn't leave with them. "Can I help you?" I ask Noel in a cold voice.

Noel crosses his arms over his massive chest and nods. "You're not staying here."

I had already figured that much out. "No worries. I'll stay with Jack."

Noel shakes his head. "Nope. You're staying with me. I can protect you better than Jack."

"Hey!" Jack yells.

"Sorry Jack, but I'm a trained police officer. I can keep her safe."

"You can't tell me what to do!" I yell and stomp my foot for good measure. "Why in the world would I want to stay with you?" I turn on Noel. All the emotion I'm feeling about my house being violated turns into anger at him for running out on our date and then not calling.

Noel looks embarrassed. "Come on, Izzy."

I raise my eyebrows at him. "Seriously, that's all you got? Screw you!" I turn to Jack. "I'll pack a bag and then we can be on our way."

I turn to go upstairs, but Noel grabs my arm. "No, Izzy. You're not listening to me. You need to stay with me so I can protect you."

I look at Noel's hand on my arm and raise my eyebrows until he releases me. "No, Noel, I don't think I do." With that, I turn and run up the stairs before I have a total meltdown.

It only takes me a minute to pack a bag with the bare minimum. I throw things in my bag haphazardly, uncaring of whether I've got the essentials or not. Looks like I'm going to be doing some shopping real soon, anyway. When I return to the living room, Noel's alone. "Where's Jack?"

"I sent him home."

"Why would you do that? Who the hell do you think you are?"

Noel is standing in front of me in a blink of an eye. "I'm your man, and I'm going to protect you," He grits out.

"Since when are you my man? Does a man run out on his woman? Does a man not call his woman?" I grunt. "You're not my man."

Noel lets his head fall forward before taking a deep breath and grabbing my face between his hands. "I fucked up, Izzy. I was embarrassed. I'm sorry." He leans his forehead against mine. "Please forgive me."

I can feel his sincerity, and I want to forgive him, but I'm just not ready yet. "I don't have the energy to deal with this right now, but I guess I'm stuck staying with you." I pick up my bag and head to the front door. I hear Noel sigh behind me, but I don't bother looking back.

Chapter 26

"I'll be Your Man" by James Blunt

I follow Noel's GTO as it thunders away through the streets to his house. I'm surprised to find that he lives in a small ranch house just minutes away from Grandma's house. He parks in his driveway and I pull up next to him. Before I can grab my bag, he opens the passenger door and snatches it. Not bad service at this hotel.

Noel motions for me to follow him through the back door. We walk straight into the kitchen. "I don't use the front door. Follow me. I'll show you to your room."

I trail behind him through the kitchen into a small, somewhat formal living room. It doesn't look like a typical bachelor pad, but maybe he's hiding a man cave in the basement. There's a hallway off of the living room, which leads to three bedrooms and a full bath. I stick my head in the bathroom and see that it's tidy and clean. Noel's house sure isn't what one would expect from an alpha male detective who drives a GTO.

Noel drops my bag on the bed in the furthest bedroom. "You can use this room while you're staying here." I nod but don't say anything. I'm still ticked at him for being Mr. Bossypants and everyone knows the silent treatment is one of a woman's best weapons in her arsenal.

"Come on," Noel says and heads to another of the bedrooms. He opens the door and it's actually an organized office. "You can work in here. You can use my computer as well. I'll text you the password."

"That's okay," I respond. "I'm going to go shopping for new equipment tomorrow." I look around the office and see a somewhat dated desktop computer. "No offense, but that computer won't work for me." I have very specific requirements for the equipment of my graphic design work.

Noel shrugs and shuts the door. "Well, the offer stands." His next words are cut off by my telephone ringing.

"Hello!" I answer.

I hear someone huff on the phone. "What is going on?" Oh, it's Betty. I should have known.

"What do you mean?"

"Don't play coy with me little missy! There were police at your house, and now you've disappeared."

I sigh. "I've hardly disappeared. I'm staying with Noel since my house was ransacked."

"Your house was ransacked! Oh, this must have something to do with Anna's murder. I'll rally the girls and we'll be right over."

"Wait! I'm at Noel's house. You can't just come barging in here!" I don't have the energy to deal with Betty and the gang at the moment.

"We'll bring extra pie." She says and hangs up before I can respond. Darn.

I look up to see Noel grinning at me. "I take it the troops are on the way." I nod and close my eyes before slumping against the wall. I don't have the energy for the old lady brigade today.

Noel rushes to me. "Are you okay?" He pulls me into his arms for a hug, and I let him. I only have so much strength to deny my hormones. Hormones basically take over your body at forty. Buyer beware.

Before I can respond to Noel's question, which I have no idea how to anyway, my phone rings again. I sigh for like the millionth time, but before I manage to move, Noel grabs the phone out of my hand and answers for me.

"Oh, hi Jack," Noel says. "Yes, we're at my house." Pause. Chuckle. "Yeah, they're on their way." Another pause. "See you then." He hangs up and hands me the phone.

"Come on," Noel says as he pulls me toward the kitchen. "I need to get some food into you before Betty and the rest of the ladies show up. You're gonna need your strength." Understatement of a lifetime.

He sits me in a chair at the table in the farm kitchen before he grabs two beers out of the refrigerator. He heats up bowls of leftover chili for us while I sip my beer. We eat in comfortable silence and are already finishing up when the doorbell rings.

"It'll be fine," Noel says to me as he goes to answer the front door. He returns to the kitchen with Betty and all the usual suspects. They're each holding a Tupperware container. I guess Betty did feel a bit bad about invading Noel's space. I've never gotten more than two containers at one time.

Betty plucks me from the chair I was sitting on and hugs me. I'm then passed around like a hot potato from one lady to the next. They all hug me and offer me words of comfort. I'm a bit dizzy by the time I manage to sit down again. Noel is grabbing plates and forks, and Ally is trying to figure out the coffee pot when the doorbell rings again.

Noel rushes off to answer it, and the ladies jump to take over his kitchen duties. Coffee mugs are found, plates and forks distributed, and the coffee started before Noel returns with Jack. Jack chuckles at the scene in front of him. "They've taken over your house," he says to Noel. Noel just shrugs in response.

Once the ladies have everything arranged to their liking, they take the chairs leaving Noel and Jack to stand. Betty grabs her notebook, and I don't even bother trying not to roll my eyes. The interrogation is about to begin.

"So," Betty says as she clicks her pen. "Fill us in on everything that's been happening since we last met."

At this point, I can't even remember what I was doing the last time I saw Betty. Noel responds on my behalf. "Maybe we should give Izzy a minute. She's had a hell of a day." Betty huffs, but puts down her pen and picks up her fork.

While we eat our pie, I tell everyone about my home invasion. Betty and Jack's ears perk up when I admit the only items, which appear to be missing are my computers and files. "So," Betty says, detective hat clearly perched back upon her head. "The burglar was looking for something."

I shrug. "I have no idea what he could have possibly been looking for." I stare Betty down. "I don't see how this could have anything to do with Grandma's death."

"It's quite the coincidence though, isn't it?" That's Jack. He's bound and determined to make this into some kind of murder mystery. I think he needs a boyfriend. Or at least I need him to have a boyfriend to distract him from ideas of murder.

I hear Noel groan and almost laugh. I can't imagine what a real detective thinks of our ragamuffin group, but it's probably not favorable.

"Anyway, did you find anything in Anna's house? What's happened?" Apparently Betty has decided to ignore the coincidence of my home invasion.

"Well, we discovered a mining company offered Grandma several million dollars for the mineral rights to her land." I hear gasps around the table. Looks like I wasn't the only one Grandma was keeping in the dark. "I talked to the conservation group as well."

Jack pipes up. "Did you learn anything new this morning, Izzy?"

"Yes, Izzy, what did you find out this morning?" Noel adds in a dark voice. I hadn't told him about my appointment, and I guess he's not exactly happy about that. I shoot him a look of apology before answering.

"It seems that the mining company was really bothering Grandma. Some rep kept coming around and phoning her – being totally pushy." I shrug. "Grandma was really bothered by it. That's why she did the whole easement thing."

"And you're only telling me about this now?" Noel's arms are crossed over his chest, and his face is thunderous. Oops. Someone's mad.

"Uh oh, someone's in trouble," Jack sings out.

Betty's all business. "What are you going to do now? Go after the mining company?"

Noel shakes his head. "No, Izzy is not going to go after the mining company. She's going to leave this matter with the professionals."

I turn on him. "What matter? What professionals? You're convinced there's no crime, remember?"

106

Noel merely shrugs, as if his previous opinion was irrelevant. "Things change. And you're in danger. I'm not letting you go snooping around anymore."

That wasn't the right thing to say. "You're not *letting* me? Who do you think you are?" I may be yelling at this point. I'm definitely standing and staring at Noel. The pissed off woman position has been assumed – hands on hips, feet shoulder width apart.

"I'm your man. And I'm keeping you safe."

I throw my hands in the air. "Stop saying you're my man! You're not my man!" I may have growled that.

Noel grabs me and pulls me tight. "I am your man. And I will keep you safe. Even if I have to keep you safe from yourself."

I wrench myself free of Noel's grip and stalk off to his spare bedroom. I really don't need his macho man crap right now. I'll sneak back to the kitchen for more pie when everyone's gone.

Chapter 27

"Barbie Girl" by Aqua

I hear Noel come into the bedroom, but it's way too early for me. I pretend I'm sleeping. He isn't buying it though, which becomes clear when he sits on the side of the bed and yanks the covers off my face.

"Hey!" What are we like twelve?

"I'm a detective. I could tell you weren't sleeping." I huff and roll to my side to give him my back. I may not be twelve years old, but I can sure act like it. He puts his hand on my shoulder and squeezes. "I wanted to make sure you were alright before I leave for work." No answer from me. I'm really good at the silent game. "Can you text me every time you go somewhere today?" I start to protest, but he doesn't let me. "I need to make sure you're safe," he says in a soft voice.

"Fine," I huff. He leans over and kisses my forehead before heading out.

I wait until I hear the roar of the GTO leaving before I get out of bed. Now that Noel woke me up, I've got places to go and people to see. I debate calling Ajax Mining to make an appointment, but then decide against it. I'm going to surprise those jerks, but first I need to replace my laptop and tablet.

Jack calls around lunchtime. "How are you?"

"I'm okay. I just finished replacing all my electronic equipment."

"That sucks."

"Yep. Luckily, I'm a millionaire nowadays," I say in a British accent, which ends up sounding like my nose is stuffed up.

Jack chuckles. "Going back to Noel's house then?"

I lower my voice and look around to see if anyone can hear me. "Nope. I'm going to go to Ajax Mining."

"Not without me you're not!" We argue for a while, but Jack is not to be dissuaded. "Fine!" I finally huff. "I'll pick you up in fifteen minutes."

Jack is waiting on his veranda when I get to his house ten minutes later. He's practically bouncing on his toes in excitement. I knew this was a bad idea. He jumps into my car with a smile on his face. "This is going to be fun," he declares.

I shake my head. "No, this is not fun. This is not a game."

"Oh, pish pash," is his only response. I let it go. I'm not in the mood to play any reindeer games with Jack.

Ajax Mining is the biggest employer in our county – maybe in Oklahoma. They have mines throughout the Plains region. This is information I learned during the past few days after googling the company. I admit I was oblivious about mining and Ajax in particular before I read Grandma's mail. The headquarters is about fifteen miles outside of town in an industrial area. The building is all modern glass and clearly designed to show off the wealth of the company. I'm impressed – not.

My nervousness builds as we walk to the building. This isn't like the conservation group. These are professionals who have harassed my grandma in an effort to feed their love of materialism and make even more money than God. I wipe my sweaty hands on my jeans in a useless effort to control my stress. I probably should have worn something more professional than a white button-down shirt, blue jeans, and shit kicker boots, although the shit kicker boots may come in handy.

A receptionist greets us as we walk into the glass atrium. "May I help you?"

"Yes," I respond. "I'd, er, we'd like to see Mr. Piers Franklin Ajax Anderson, please." What an obnoxious name!

The receptionist looks surprised but quickly covers it. "What is this concerning?"

"He wrote several letters to my grandmother about the mineral rights to her land," I respond simply. No sense accusing him of anything until I can look him in the eye. My natural feminine ability to know when a man is lying is honed to perfection after ten years of marriage to Ryan, who lied to cover up his adrenalin-junkie habits when he realized how irritated paying for his exploits made me.

"Please have a seat," she says and points us to a lounge area. "Can I bring you anything to drink?" I merely shake my head.

While we wait, Jack tuts at the fashion faux pas in the corporate world. "Do they know colors exist?" he whispers as a group of workers, dressed solely in blacks and grays, return from a smoking break. When he starts to point out the most egregious mistakes, I slap his hand and tell him to hush. "We're not here for a fashion show," I hiss. Luckily, the receptionist chooses that moment to call us over.

"Here are your badges for entry. Go to the furthest elevator and take it to the 20th floor. Someone will meet you there."

The furthest elevator only goes to the 20th floor. A well-manicured blonde Barbie mannequin is waiting for us when the elevator doors open. She looks down her nose at us before turning around. She doesn't even deign to speak to us. I look at Jack and mouth "Wow" before following her. Jack can't stop staring at her shoes – pink stilettos with sparkles. He's probably wondering where she bought them. I, on the other hand, am more fascinated by her utterly perfect physique. I don't think I've ever seen anyone in person who is so flawlessly put together. Double wow.

I hear a door shut behind me and turn to look. I see the back of a man entering the stairwell. From behind he looks exactly like Noel, but before I can be sure, the door shuts after him and I lose sight of him. I shrug, probably just another tall man with dark hair. There's no reason to think Noel would be here.

Barbie leads us to a corner office. She knocks lightly on the door before pushing it open. "Mr. Ajax." An elderly man, who has obviously enjoyed his meals a bit too much, stands from behind a massive oak desk. "Thank you, Lindsay," he says before turning to us. His smile looks genuine and puts me immediately at ease. "Please have a seat." He gestures to the leather chairs in front of his desk before sitting again. "How may I help you?"

"Are you Mr. Piers Franklin Ajax Anderson?" I ask as we sit.

He shakes his head. "No, I'm Alex Ajax. Piers is my nephew. Why are you asking for him?" I could swear he wrinkles his nose when he says nephew, but the action is so swift I may be imagining things.

I pull the letter out of my bag. Luckily, I had this letter along with the other legal documents I received from the law firm in my bag when my house was ransacked. "He wrote to my grandmother and offered her several million dollars for the mineral rights on her land," I respond.

Mr. Ajax motions for the letter, and I reach across the desk to hand it to him. He grabs a pair of reading glasses from his desk and quickly scans the letter before handing it back. "This is just a standard acquisition letter. I don't understand the issue."

I take a deep breath before proceeding. I'm not really in the habit of accusing people of harassment. I don't even know if what Mr. Anderson did was a crime, but here goes. "The man who wrote this letter harassed my grandmother. Grandma told him she wasn't interested, but he kept calling and dropping by bothering her."

Mr. Ajax is obviously uncomfortable. His face turns pink and he squirms a bit in his seat before he clears his throat and leans forward. "I'm sorry to hear about that. I can assure you, your grandmother won't be bothered anymore. Mr. Anderson no longer works for Ajax Mining."

Well, shoot, I hadn't expected that answer. Now what? "Why not?" Jack asks before I have a chance to gather my wits about me.

"Excuse me?" Mr. Ajax gives Jack a look of contempt.

Jack isn't bothered and plows forward. "We have a right to know if you handled this situation properly. Maybe we should consult with our lawyers." He actually pretends to stand up as if he's going to stomp out of the office. I always knew he was a good actor.

Mr. Ajax huffs. "I assure you Ajax Mining has handled this situation properly and with the utmost speed. Your grandmother will no longer be bothered by Mr. Anderson."

"When was Mr. Anderson fired?"

"Not that it's any of your business, but Mr. Anderson stopped working for Ajax Mining months ago." Mr. Ajax stands, obviously done with this line of questioning and with us. "Now, if you'll excuse me, I have a multi-billionaire dollar company to run."

I try to save face by thanking Mr. Ajax, but he ignores us and goes back to the paperwork on his desk. Lindsay is already waiting for us at the door to his office. She shakes her head at us as if we're some vermin needing to be exterminated, but her boobs remain still and are perfectly perky.

Back in the car, Jack is buzzing with excitement. "Mr. Anderson did it. I just know it!"

"You know no such thing," I say as I start the car and head back to town, but I'm secretly plotting how I can investigate Mr. I-need-four-names-to-show-how-important-I-am.

Chapter 28

"I Can't Drive 55" by Sammy Hagar

"Izzy," Jack says when we're about halfway to town. "That car has been following us since we left Ajax Mining."

"Don't be silly Jack. There's only one main road between the company and town. Anyone leaving the company would take this road into town." Just to be sure I sneak a peek behind us. Sure enough, there is a car on my rear bumper, which is a bit odd as I'm driving – quick peek at the speedometer – about 15 miles over the speed limit. Oops!

"I'll slow down and he'll pass," I say as we enter a long, straight stretch of road. We've got lots of flat road in Oklahoma. I drop my speed to five miles under the limit and open my window to wave him ahead of us, but he doesn't take the bait.

"What the…" I say as he continues riding my bumper, seemingly uncaring about the speed I'm driving.

"Izzy, I don't like this." Jack is clearly nervous. He's holding onto the *oh shit* bar with both hands and constantly looking back to check on the car.

"No worries. I'll turn off, he'll continue straight and that'll be that." I hope.

I see a turnoff for a secondary road coming up and turn on my blinker to take the turn. After I've turned, I look back and see a Chevy Impala barreling closer toward us.

"Oh shit, Izzy, he's still following us."

"Calm down Jack. You're not helping. We've driven these roads a million times. We'll lose him." Too bad I'm not driving Noel's GTO right now. I could lose the jerk in no time.

"Hang on," I yell, but I don't really need to. Jack's hands are now permanently attached to the *oh shit* bar. I take a left without slowing down. My rear end fishtails a bit, but I quickly bring the car back under my control. I hear tires squeal behind and take a quick peek. Still behind us.

"Can you see his license plate number?" Jack becomes a contortionist as he twists and twirls himself around to look at the license plate of our pursuer without letting go of the handle.

"I got it," Jack declares.

"Well, what are you waiting for? Write it down!"

"I'll remember," he says, but I grunt. "No, you won't! Make a note in your phone or something." Grumbling, Jack finally lets go of the handle to grab his phone. I try to keep the car steady as he does. When he finishes and grabs hold of the *oh shit* bar once again, I punch the gas.

"Fuck, Izzy! What are we gonna do?" Jack is completely panicked now.

"We'll lose him. It's only another five miles into town. If we don't lose him before then, we'll drive straight to the police station." I sound confident because I actually feel confident. I may not be good at many things, but I can drive the hell out of a car. Having been married to a daredevil has its advantages, although I might have been a bit of a speed demon before I even met Ryan.

I slow down just enough to take a sharp right. The land here is completely flat and roads are laid out like a grid with ninety-degree corners. I've practiced taking corners at high speeds since I got my driver's license. Jack and I used to come out here joyriding in high school all the time. I thought I was a pretty good driver until I met Ryan. Ryan had no fear. You can drive really fast if you're not afraid of anything.

Tires squealing behind me let me know that our pursuer is still around. I take another quick left turn, hoping he'll shoot by the intersection. No such luck, he's still behind us. The dust kicking up from driving on these back roads isn't helping to try and evade him.

"Hold on," I tell Jack.

"I am holding on!" he screams in return.

"It might get a bit hairy now," I tell him. "I can't lose him, so I'm just going to drive like the devil to the police station."

"Are you out of your mind?"

I smile and take a quick peek at Jack. "Maybe." It's a straight shot into town. I can easily get up to a speed of 100 miles per hour. The muscle car roaring behind us can meet that speed and exceed it, but I know these roads like the back of my hand.

I floor the gas and concentrate on the road in front of me, praying there's no one else on this route. There's not much traffic on this secondary highway, but there's always a chance of a tractor or combine coming out of nowhere. Considering the size and speed of farming equipment, that would be a complete disaster.

Luck is on our side. We make it to the city limits without running into any traffic – farming or otherwise. Our chaser is still on my tail, but I notice him slow and give me more space once I'm on the main drag. I pull into the police station. I exhale when I see the Impala continue past us. I try to catch a glimpse of the driver, but I'm too late. I think I see a blur of white. I'm not sure though.

Jack and I sit in the car for a minute to calm down and catch our breath. "You didn't pee your pants, did you?" I tease Jack as his breathing finally starts to become normal.

"Ha! Ha! Very funny. You drive like a freaking maniac!"

"Learned from the best," I say and wink at him. Jack is a speed demon as well. He just doesn't like anyone else driving.

"Come on," I say as I climb out of the car. As much as I don't want to, I know I need to report this incident to the police. Noel is going to be livid but so be it.

Just my luck. When I walk into the police station, the officer I reported – or tried to report – Grandma's murder to is standing at the front desk. He recognizes me immediately. "What relative do you think was murdered now?" he asks and then guffaws loudly. Jack looks at me in confusion, but I just shake my head in reply.

I look around the police station, but Noel doesn't seem to be around. Phew. I clear my throat. "Actually, we were just in a car chase. Someone was following us."

The officer only blinks in reply. Finally, he grunts and motions us to the back. "You'd better come back then."

Jack and I follow the officer to an interrogation room. The cop tells us to sit, and that he'll be right back. He doesn't shut the door on his way out, and I can't help but hear his next words.

"It's that chick that Noel's dating." I bristle at the word chick. "Noel said she's on some wild goose chase. Thinks her grandma was murdered or something." I feel my cheeks warm with embarrassment and strain to hear the rest of the conversation. "We're supposed to report anything suspicious about that mining company to Noel." I hear footsteps move away.

Jack and I stare at each other in surprise, wondering what the heck that was about. Another police officer arriving, this time a woman, cuts off any discussion. She sits across from us and dumps a large pile of papers in front of her.

"So," she begins. "Tell me what happened."

Officer Donavon, turns out that's her name, listens carefully to our story. She asks a few questions about locations and speed we were driving, but otherwise doesn't interrupt me. Afterward, she has us fill out a few reports before heading out to run the plates.

The second she leaves the room, I turn to Jack and whisper. "What do you think those cops were talking about?"

Jack shrugs. "I wouldn't read much into it. I'm sure Noel doesn't think you're on a wild goose chase anymore."

I shake my head. "No, not about that." I lean forward. "About Noel wanting anything that happens with the mining company to be reported to him. What do you think that's about?"

Jack doesn't get a chance to respond as Officer Donavon returns. She shuts the door and sits down. "There's no license plate with the number 481 HDX registered in Oklahoma." She looks at Jack. "You sure it was an Oklahoma plate?"

Jack bristles. "Of course I'm sure. I've lived here my entire life. It was an O.K. plate: Native America written across the bottom and a man shooting a bow on the left."

The officer nods. "Okay, we'll have to run the make and model of the car and see if we come up with anything similar. It

116

will take a while." She stands. "You guys can go. We'll call if we hear anything."

Jack and I scurry out of the police station as if we were grade schoolers and the recess bell just rang.

Chapter 29

"Do You Want to Know a Secret?" by The Beatles

Jack and I are anxious on the drive to his house. We both check the mirrors constantly. Luckily, we don't see anyone following us. "You sure you'll be okay on your own," I ask when we reach Jack's house.

"I'll be fine," Jack responds and places a kiss on my forehead before hopping out of the car.

Noel's GTO is parked in the driveway when I arrive. Darn. I last texted him at noon to tell him I was going to Jack's. If he stopped by Jack's house, I'm screwed. When I open the back door, Noel is sitting in the kitchen nursing a beer. He looks angry. Double darn.

"Hey," I say cautiously. "How was your day?"

"How was my day?" His voice is dark and low. "Is that what you wanna go with? How was my fucking day?"

I sigh and sit down across from him at the kitchen table. "What do you want to know?" I ask. No longer pretending I haven't been up to no good.

"How about why didn't you call me when you thought you were being followed? I really enjoyed getting a phone call from the station that you were there to report an incident." He's seething now. I don't bother to answer. There is no correct answer to this. "And, oh, where were you all afternoon? Because you sure as shit weren't at Jack's house."

Noel stands and throws his empty beer bottle in the trash before grabbing a new one from the frig. He sits down across from me before draining half the beer in one gulp. I think I'm going to need a few of those to settle my nerves before dealing with pissed-off-Noel.

"Do you maybe wanna talk about this when you've calmed down some?" I dare to ask. Noel just throws me a wicked glare. "Ok, fine," I say and throw my hands up in surrender. I stand and grab a beer from the frig as well.

After I take an extremely large, not lady like at all, gulp, I look at Noel and answer his second question. "We went to Ajax Mining," I say and wait for the explosion. It doesn't take long.

"You what?" Noel's face is red as he jumps from his chair and starts pacing the kitchen. "I specifically told you not to go there."

I know he's mad because he's worried about me, but ordering me around is not okay. I stand and face him. "You can't order me around," I grit out.

"Yes. I. Can." He enunciates each word slowly and clearly as if he's talking to a preschooler. "I'm your man," he holds up a hand to stop my response to his caveman-like antics. "And even if I weren't, I'm a police officer. If I order you to do something or not to do something, you need to listen to me."

"I was never good at taking orders." I'm flippant now. I don't want to have the same fight again and again.

"That's clear," Noel says as he collapses in his chair. "So what happened?"

I clear my throat. "Well, the guy that was harassing Grandma no longer works at the company."

"Give me his name and I'll check him out." I write the name down on a piece of paper and hand it to Noel.

"And you were followed?" I nod. "Why do you think you were followed?"

I describe the car chase to him. Noel's face loses more and more color as I continue. He jumps from his chair and pulls me out of mine for a hug when I finish. "Fuck, baby, you could have been hurt." He squeezes me.

"I'm fine," I can barely speak. He just holds me tight. After a few minutes, he loosens his grip to look me in the eyes.

"You are fine, aren't you?"

"It was fun," I say, and he groans.

"What am I going to do with you?"

I shrug. "I don't know, but it will probably be a ball."

119

Noel throws his head back and laughs. "Yeah," he nods. "If I don't have a heart attack first."

I consider asking Noel about what the police officers were talking about. Why does he want any incidents regarding Ajax Mining to be reported to him? But I quickly give up on the idea. One angry outburst from Noel per day is my limit. I head off to take a shower and wash the grime of yet another trip to the police station off me.

When I come out of the shower, I'm surprised to hear laughing and joking in the kitchen. Is this Noel's poker night? I quickly dress in yoga pants and a t-shirt before heading toward the noise. I stop in my tracks at the door to the kitchen. The gang's all here – Jack along with Betty and her entourage.

"What's going on?" I ask Noel, who's looking mighty guilty.

"I called a meeting," he responds. I raise my eyebrows at him, but he ignores my unspoken questions. "Have a seat. Betty brought dinner."

I quickly sit. I can get mad at whatever Noel's scheming afterwards. Betty may be a master when it comes to baking, but her cooking is out of this world. We eat quickly and the ladies wash up. I try to stand to help, but Martha and Rose give me dirty looks. Okay, guess I'm staying seated then. Noel comes over and lifts me up before sitting down and gathering me into his lap.

"Okay, ladies. I want to talk about why I asked everyone to come over," Noel starts. I try really hard, really I do, but I can't stop the loud sigh that leaves my mouth. Noel hugs me closer, but otherwise doesn't respond to my obvious annoyance.

"As everyone knows, Izzy and Jack were followed today." The ladies nod, grim and serious for once. "This is dangerous. Your merry band of investigators has to stop snooping around before someone gets hurt."

Everyone nods and agrees while I bristle. I can't believe everyone is giving up just like that. What the heck? I thought the white-haired lady clique would be stronger than this. I mean, what do they have to worry about? They've lived full lives. It's twilight time for them anyway. I don't understand Jack either. He was all excited about this detective work. Maybe the car chase scared him more than he's willing to admit?

I give Jack the evil eye, but he winks and puts his finger in front of his mouth in a shush motion. Okay, now I'm really confused. Betty pipes up. "Noel, we completely understand. We don't want Izzy to be in any danger." She sounds serious.

Ally brings out a chocolate cake. Now things are really getting weird. I beg Ally to make her chocolate cake all the time. She almost always refuses. She claims it takes hours to make and only bakes it on special occasions. Is she trying to sweeten me or Noel up? Not that I'm unthankful for the cake or anything.

By the time Jack and the ladies leave, I'm exhausted and head straight to bed after giving Noel a quick peck on the cheek. I'm irritated with him for convening the coven and giving us orders, but I'm too tired to call him on it.

Chapter 30

"Do You Want to Know a Secret?" by The Beatles

I hear Noel leave early the next morning, but I'm feeling depressed and have lost any motivation to get out of bed. So I don't. I roll over and fall back asleep. A phone ringing on my bedside table wakes me up a few hours later.

"Hello," I say, but I'm a bit groggy and it probably comes out sounding like *whello.*

"Izzy? Are you still in bed?" I jump straight up and out of bed. Nothing like a grandmother guilting you about being lazy.

"Um no." I lie.

"Anyway," Betty ignores my lie. "We're getting together this morning to research that Mr. Anderson on the line."

"Okay," I answer trying to understand what's going on. Didn't she agree yesterday to give up her Jessica Fletcher ways?

"It turns out that none of us actually is on the line at home." I pull a pillow in front of my face and snicker into it. "We don't want to go to the library," Betty continues as if she hasn't heard me snickering. "We need to do this on the low down."

"I think you mean down low," I can't help myself from saying.

"Yes, yes down low. Anyway," she continues in a rush, uncaring about correct terminology. "We need your help. Can you get us on the line?"

I may be forty and therefore born before children came out of the uterus attached to tablets, but I can handle the simple assignment of getting the ladies online. "But wait a minute," I say, no longer able to keep my confusion quiet about the turn of events. "I thought you agreed with Noel. You weren't going to do any more snooping, remember?"

Betty laughs. "Of course we told your nice young man that. We didn't want to upset him."

I snicker. Noel is over forty and weighs something like 250 pounds. She makes it sound like he's a lanky teenager trying to pretend he's a man. I love it. Of course I'm in! "Where are we meeting?"

I'm not surprised to see Jack's car parked in front of Betty's house when I arrive thirty minutes later. "Don't you ever work?" I ask him when he opens the front door knowing full well he does as he pleases. Jack doesn't deign to answer me; merely shows me to the kitchen table where the ladies are gathered around an ancient desktop computer. I look back at Jack, who's trying not to laugh. I don't think the computer is even plugged in. Good thing I came prepared!

I haul my brand spanking new laptop out of my messenger bag and motion to Jack. "Can you get rid of the antique?"

"It will be my pleasure." He bows before whispering into my ear, "Seriously, can I throw it away?" I shake my head. Jack is probably more offended by the lack of style of the desktop than its lack of usefulness.

I start up my computer and the ladies all gather around behind me.

"Wow, that's so much prettier than yours Betty," Ally says, and I hear Jack laugh.

"Oooh, and it works too. Look, there are pictures opening up," Martha adds.

I clear my throat before Betty goes Mike Tyson on them. "What do we want to know about Piers Franklin Ajax Anderson?"

Betty pulls out her trusty notebook. I wouldn't be surprised if she was a spy in a previous life or something. "Well, obviously, we need to know where he lives, where he comes from, how long he worked at the mining company. Stuff like that."

I google the name and all kinds of stuff pops up. The Ajax family is incredibly wealthy, like Richie Rich wealthy. Their names are all over the society pages. Every time they give money to charity or play golf, there's an article in the gossip column about it. They probably can't fart without some paparazzi wanting to write about it. I shiver. That's no way to live.

There's less information about Piers Anderson, but I know he's the nephew of the current CEO of Ajax Mining. With a little more digging, we find out he's the son of Alex Ajax's sister, Barbra Chelsey Ajax Anderson. This family obviously loves pretentious names. Her other sons feature prominently in the society pages and are members of the board at Ajax Mining.

"That's weird," Rosemary says when our search of the society columns pitters out. "The other family members are all over these pages. It's almost like Piers Anderson doesn't exist."

"I'll tell you why," Jack pipes up and we all turn to hear him out. "He's obviously the bad boy of his family. He could be gay and they're ashamed of him." We all titter in indignation. "Or he's just a troublemaker." He shrugs.

"Sounds about right," I agree. "What now?"

Betty looks around and then motions for everyone to come closer. "Let's go search his house," she whispers.

I nearly fall off my chair. Betty, the knitting buddy of my grandma who has arthritis in her knees and bakes like a god, just suggested we do a home invasion. But wait – it gets better. Ally, Rosemary, Martha, and Rose agree with her. They're all nodding their heads and smiling in anticipation. I look to Jack to reason with them, but he too is nodding his head.

"Have you all gone crazy?" I shout.

"Shhh," Betty says as if worried someone will overhear us. "What's the big deal?"

"Well, the last time I searched someone's house I ended up in the back seat of a police car. Not something I really want to repeat." I shake my head at their obvious descent into madness.

"But it's not like you had to spend the night in jail or anything, was it?" Ally pipes in. "Noel got you out of trouble."

The other ladies nod in agreement. "Yeah, Noel will keep our backs safe," Rosemary says.

"Um, ladies, this is the same man who told you to back off yesterday." What in the world is going on? Since when am I the voice of reason?

The ladies tut. "It's fine. He loves you. He won't let anything happen. He'll be mad, but he'll get over it."

Somehow I end up agreeing to stage a home invasion tonight. How did that happen? Did the ladies lace my coffee with something? I've clearly lost my mind.

Chapter 31

"Thieves in the Temple" by Prince

Luckily Noel has to work this evening and so there's no need for lying or subterfuge on my part. Although I'm an awesome liar, er, wielder of tall tales if I do say so myself. I wait until I hear the rumble of Noel's GTO leave before jumping into my car and heading to Rosemary's house. We discovered this afternoon that Piers Anderson only lives a few blocks from Rosemary.

I walk into Rosemary's house but am stopped short when I see the ensemble of merry thieves in front of me. I'm dressed in black jeans, black t-shirt, and a dark blue hoodie. I couldn't find any dark colored sports shoes so I'm wearing black ballet flats. Jack, on the other hand, is wearing a catsuit. Yes, a catsuit. And he's grinning like the Cheshire Cat.

When I stop to stare at Jack, he strikes a pose. "You like?" He asks.

"I don't even know how to answer that question," I respond. Instead, I check out Betty and her merry band of thieves. They too are dressed mostly in black. Apparently, however, orthopedic shoes only come in bright white. Between those shoes and the almost fluorescent bluish white hair of the ladies, I wonder what in the heck I'm doing.

Betty seems to read my mind and shows me her scarf. The other ladies follow suit and quickly tie scarves around their heads. Indeed, they are less obvious now if we were going to a cat burglar convention for the elderly and insane.

"What are people going to think when they see us walking through the neighborhood?" My eyes are wide and I'm trying not to stare and offend anyone, but it's hard work.

"Just that we're out for an evening stroll with the dog," Rosemary answers.

"There's a bit of a problem with that idea." I pause and the ladies wait. "We don't have a freaking dog!"

"Fido's a free spirit." Jack's not missing a beat.

"And another thing's bothering me."

Betty sighs at me as if she's a long-suffering mother putting up with a delinquent child. "Why does Piers Anderson live in this area? He's a millionaire with a huge trust fund. No offense, Rosemary, but this isn't exactly a wealthy neighborhood." Rosemary smiles at me to indicate she isn't offended.

"That's what we're here to find out." Betty rubs her hands in excitement. I'm officially in trouble now.

"How are we actually going to get in his house when we get there?" We really haven't researched this breaking and entering evening thoroughly. I'm sure some YouTube videos would have helped had I thought about the actual logistics of the evening. Instead, I'm completely terrified I'm going to end up at the police station – again. Whether I'm dating Noel or not won't matter if we get caught red handed.

"We'll figure something out," Betty says and starts to walk through the door. The discussion is apparently finished.

We stroll through the neighborhood until we get to Piers Anderson's block. I'm looking around making sure no one is interested in what we're up to, but apparently all the neighborhood busybodies are accompanying me on my evening of breaking and entering. Unlike me, Jack and Betty look like eager beavers. Their smiles are so bright they make the black clothing we're wearing completely superfluous. I was already anxious about breaking into someone's house, but now I'm also worried about what those two will get up to.

Betty brings everyone into a huddle in front of the house next to Anderson's place. "Okay, this is what we're going to do," she whispers. Oh great, she's got a plan to get us into even more trouble. "Jack and Izzy are going to go around back and see if they can find a way in the house. Rose and I will try the front. Ally and Martha will stand guard." Everyone nods eagerly. There must not be a good episode of *Matlock* on tonight. "Bark if you run into any trouble."

"Did you say bark?" I ask, but shake my head not waiting for an answer.

Jack grabs my hand and we're off. Anderson's house is a dump. Seriously, a dump. The yard is overgrown and looks like a jungle. Paint is peeling from the walls and windows. There are no curtains or blinds. Instead, newspaper is taped to the inside of the windows. I can't help but worry why Piers is so darn determined to ensure no one can see in his house. What is he hiding in there?

Jack pulls me away from my perusal of the house toward the driveway. He slowly tiptoes and hunches over as he walks. It would be funny if I weren't terrified. We swerve behind the garage. There's a broken window on the side of the building, and I peek in. Except for a car, which is mostly covered with a large sheet, the building is completely empty. There's not even a trash can. A bit odd, but nothing illegal.

We continue to walk around the building, but something about the car's shape hidden under the sheet is triggering a memory. "Hey Jack," I whisper. "Why do I know that car?" He shrugs and puts his finger over his mouth to shush me.

Believe it or not, the backyard is actually worse than the front. In addition to the jungle theme, there are various tools and some furniture lying around rotting. We have to be careful not to trip. I wonder if my tetanus shot is up-to-date. The windows at the back of the house aren't covered by newspaper, and light is pouring out from them. Uh oh, someone's home.

I pull on Jack's arm. "Someone's here, Jack. Let's go." He ignores me and heads toward a window at the end of the house. This corner of the building is dark and just a tad bit scary. Did I mention creepy? Because this house is all kinds of creepy.

I hear a sound similar to a dog bark and start turning around, but Jack is still holding my hand and refuses to let me go. He's quite the determined delinquent. We reach the window, but despite Jack's height, he can't see in. He jumps up, but the window's too high. Without a word, he lets go of my hand, crouches down, and interlaces his fingers. I just stare at him.

"Come on, Izzy," he begs. "If I give you a boost, you can see in." I continue to stand there. I give him my, *you've got to be freaking crazy look*, but it's dark and he doesn't notice. There's also the possibility he's ignoring me. Finally, I huff and put my right foot in Jack's hand. He lifts me up and I put my hands on his shoulders to steady myself.

I take a deep breath before peering into the window. It's a bedroom and not a very nice one at that. There's a mattress on the floor, but no bed frame. Clothes are strewn about the room. I'm about to make Jack let me down when a man walks into the room. Oh shit. The light from the hallway doesn't offer enough illumination for me to make out any of his features. He's muttering to himself and kicking at the clothes on the floor.

I'm panicking and trying to get Jack to lower me when the man looks up and stares at me. Can he see me? He stalks towards the window. I scream, and he lunges forward.

Jack immediately pulls me down and into his arms. He rushes off around the house and runs down the street as fast as he can. Good thing he's tall and in shape. We continue for a block and then he lets me down. He grabs my hand and takes off again. We don't stop until we get to Rosemary's house.

We stand on the porch catching our breath and waiting for the ladies to join us. After what seems like an eternity, they arrive.

"Did he see you? Did anyone follow you?" Jack shouts to Betty while she's still on the sidewalk. She shakes her head in response. "Thank God," Jack says and falls against the side of the house. I squeeze his hand and pull him into the house that Rosemary has now unlocked.

"What happened?" Betty asks once we are ensconced at the kitchen table.

I shiver. "Someone was in the house. He saw me and lunged at me before Jack pulled me down and we ran out of there." I'm completely freaked out.

"Did you get a look at him?" Jack asks.

I shake my head. "No. It was too dark to see."

"What are we going to do now?" Ally asks.

I shrug and stand. "I don't know, but I'm going home."

Noel isn't home when I arrive at his house. I shrug off my jeans and sweatshirt and throw them on the floor. Too tired for pajamas, I crawl into bed in my black t-shirt and fall asleep immediately.

Chapter 32

"Enter Sandman" by Metallica

"AAAAAHHH," I wake screaming and Noel pulls me into his arms.

"Shhh," he murmurs as he strokes my hair.

"What's going on? Why are you in my bed?" I'm disorientated and confused. My heart is pounding a million beats a minute.

"You were having a nightmare," Noel whispers. "I crawled into bed with you to calm you down and fell asleep." He shrugs and hugs me closer.

I turn in his arms to face him. "You feel asleep?" Sounds about as truthful as the ever popular, *I ran out of gas* ruse.

I didn't pull the shades down when I went to bed last night and the moonlight is bright enough to illuminate Noel's blushing face. "This is where I want to be. Shoot me for taking advantage of any opportunity that comes along."

I sigh. "But why?"

"Why what?" He looks confused.

"Why do you want to be here? Why me?" I use my hand to indicate the connection between us.

"Didn't we already discuss this?" I shrug. "Because I like you. Hell, I think I started falling in love with you the moment I saw you." He laughs. "You were so gorgeous and completely embarrassed when I called you out for using your feminine wiles to get service. I was dreading that night, but one look at you and I would have suffered through hundreds of speed dates for just another look. You looked at me and made me laugh. That's all it took."

Wow! That's super sweet and utterly terrifying. "I'm scared. I haven't... you know," I clear my throat. "...been with anyone since..."

"Sshhh." Noel reaches up and places one finger over my lips. "That's okay. We'll take things slow."

I smile and snuggle into Noel's arms. My breathing goes back to normal and my heart is no longer in danger of jumping out of my chest. "Now, what are these nightmares about? Is it the car chase?" Noel asks before I can fall asleep.

Shit. I'm going to have to tell Noel about last night's little adventure. He's going to be livid. "Promise you won't get mad."

"I can't promise that," he says as he shifts back so he can look me in the eyes.

I squirm. "Can you at least promise not to go ballistic then?"

A long-suffering sigh. "Fine."

"We kinda sorta snooped around Piers Anderson's house tonight," I speak softly, hoping he won't hear me.

Noel jumps out of bed and stares me down. "You what?" I think he heard me.

I shrug my shoulders. "It wasn't my idea. Betty started it." I sound like a two-year-old.

"Betty should have an armed guard," Noel mutters. "What happened?" His arms are crossed over his bare chest - which incidentally looks yummy - and his feet are planted shoulder width apart. He's livid.

"Not much actually. We went around to his house. Which is a complete dump, by the way. Jack and I went around the back. Jack gave me a lift and I peeked into the bedroom. Guy came into the bedroom. I freaked out and screamed. Jack and I ran out of there like we had ants in our pants. End of story."

Noel runs a hand through his hair in frustration. "Okay, that doesn't sound too bad. Why are you having nightmares?"

I shiver. "That man scared the bejesus out of me. When he saw me, it's like he was a hunter and I was his prey. He stalked toward me." I shiver again. "It was freaky."

Noel comes back to the bed and kneels in front of me. "Do you know him?"

I shrug. "I couldn't really see him."

"Could he be the man in the car that was chasing you?"

I shake my head. "No, I couldn't see who was in the car. The windows were tinted." I stop. Something's nagging at me. Some whisper of a memory. "Huh, I wonder."

"What?"

"There was a car in the garage at Piers Anderson's house. It was covered with a tarp, but something about the shape looked really familiar." I jump up and clap. "That's it! It's the same car." Noel looks confused. "The car in the garage is the same car that chased us. I'm sure of it. I even asked Jack if the car was familiar. I knew it right away! Well, I knew it, but I didn't know I knew it. You know what I mean."

"I'll check into it in the morning. The police report will have the description and the license plate number." He smiles and pulls me back into bed. "Now, let's get some sleep. Unless you're going to have another revelation."

I shake my head and settle into his arms. A girl could get used to this.

Chapter 33

"Why Can't This Be Love" by Van Halen

Noel's gone when I wake in the morning. It's still dark and I'm wondering why in the world I'm awake when I hear the beep from my phone indicating a voice mail. Man, I must have been sleeping pretty deep to miss Noel leaving and my phone ringing.

The voice mail is from Betty. I don't bother to listen to it, but call her instead. It's never a good sign when someone, let alone an elderly person, calls before the butt crack of dawn. "Is everything okay?" I ask without preamble.

"You're not going to believe it!" Betty's voice is high from excitement. What now?

"What's that Betty?" I try not to sound like the long-suffering child.

"They've got Mr. Anderson in custody!"

"What?" I bolt out of bed. "How do you know that?"

"I have a police scanner, of course," Betty's voice sounds proud. I should have known.

"Anyway, what happened?"

"Someone was snooping around your house and the police picked him up. Turns out it was Mr. Anderson! Pick me up in ten minutes."

"Wait – what? Why am I picking you up?"

"Because my car's in the shop." Now it's Betty's turn to sigh and sound long-suffering.

"Um, where are we going?"

"To the police station, of course!"

The woman has gone crazy. There's no way in hell I'm going to the police and bothering them during an ongoing investigation. She's out of her mind. And that's exactly what I tell her. "You're out of your mind. I'm not going to the police station."

133

"Fine," she huffs. "I'll just call Ally." This is going to get out of hand quickly if I don't stop it. The merry band of old lady thieves is going to descend on the police station and cause chaos. Noel will kill me if that happens.

"I'll call Noel and ask him to fill us in. How's that sound?" I offer as a compromise. Betty agrees to wait to storm the police and I immediately call Noel, but his phone goes to voicemail. Probably because he's playing bad cop and interrogating Mr. Anderson. If I don't do anything, he's going to be pissed when the ladies show up at the station. I take extreme action. I text Noel 911.

The phone rings a few minutes later. Thank God. I don't think I – or Noel's carpet – could have survived much longer. "What's wrong?" Noel answers sounding breathless.

"We have a problem," I start. "Betty heard about Mr. Anderson's arrest on her police scanner, and now she's determined to gather the troops and head on over to the police station."

Noel lets out a string of obscenities a sailor would be proud of. "You need to stop her."

"That's what I'm trying to do. Anything you can give me."

Sigh. "Not yet. I'll try to keep you informed though. Do you think that will hold Betty off?"

"I'll make it sound better than that, but yeah."

"Love you," he says and hangs up the phone. Wait! What? Did he just use the L-word for the first time? On the phone? And as a secondary thought? I don't have time to think about it as my phone is already blowing up. It's Jack.

"What's going on, Iz? Betty's calling me telling me I need to take her to the police station. Is everything okay?"

I slump into a chair. "Everything's fine. The police arrested Mr. Anderson for snooping around my house this morning, and of course, Betty heard about it on the police scanner and wants to invade the police station and question him herself."

Jack chuckles. "Noel would love that."

"I just talked to him. He basically begged me to do everything in my power to stop her and the troops."

"What are you gonna do?"

"I'll invite everyone over here. Noel will keep us as informed as much as possible. Hopefully, that will satisfy the gang."

Before I even manage to hang up with Jack, the doorbell is ringing. I open the door and to my not-so-great surprise find Betty, Rosemary, Ally, Martha, and Rose on the stoop. I usher everyone into the kitchen. Ally's carrying grocery bags. At least I'm going to get fed.

The ladies make a breakfast buffet that would make a Michelin-starred restaurant jealous – sausage, pancakes, fluffy eggs. There's even cinnamon buns with homemade icing. Jack arrives during the preparations. He's no dummy.

While we eat, the ladies speculate about Mr. Anderson and what he's up to. Rose is convinced he's a serial killer – although she's not certain why cereal is involved. Martha thinks he's obsessed with me. Ally and Rosemary agree. Betty is still working the angles on why Piers would kill Grandma. Needless to say, breakfast is freaking exhausting, even if it is super yummy.

"Why haven't we heard anything from Noel yet?" Betty inquires while looking at her watch. "It's been two hours now."

I don't think two hours is enough time to interrogate someone, but what do I know? To keep the old lady brigade calm, I text Noel for some information.

The natives are getting restless. Update?

It only takes a minute for Noel to respond.

Charging Anderson w/B&E of your place. That enough?

I relay the information to the ladies before another text comes through.

Please tell me that's enough.

I respond: **Natives under control. Out.**

Ally, Rosemary, and Martha are convinced this news corroborates their theory that Anderson is obsessed with me while Betty and Rose are unconvinced. It's exhausting listening to them. I wonder if *Matlock* or *Murder, She wrote* are on Netflix. Wait, better not encourage their amateur sleuthing.

While the ladies are distracted with cleaning up, I grab Jack and head to my bedroom. I shut the door before turning to him.

"What's going on?" He asks with one eyebrow raised.

I can barely breathe, but I've got to tell Jack. "Noel said the L-word," I whisper.

Jack jumps up and down and claps. "Yeah," he shouts.

"Shhhh," I hush him before the ladies invade my bedroom.

"He just said it as an afterthought when we hung up on the phone. Does that count?" I chew on my nail as I stare at him, waiting for an answer.

"Of course it counts." He rolls his eyes at me.

"Do you think he loves me?" I stare at the floor, afraid to look into Jack's eyes.

Jack grabs my cheeks between his hands and tilts my head to face him. "Everyone can see he loves you, but you. He looks at you like you hang the moon. For him, you do."

A wide smile breaks out on my face and I jump into Jack's arms. "Thanks," I murmur into his shoulder.

"Izzy," I hear shouted from the kitchen.

"Come on," Jack lets me go and opens the bedroom door. "The troops are getting antsy."

Chapter 34

"Guilty" by Joe Cocker

I manage to find some *Columbo* episodes on Netflix but, after two episodes, the ladies have just about had it with waiting. Betty is threatening to go to the police station when I hear a knock. I jump up and run to the door in time to beat Betty.

I'm shocked to see a police officer on Noel's porch when I open the door. "Can I help you? Detective Blackburn isn't here."

The cop smiles. "Detective Blackburn sent me." I raise my eyebrows in question. "He wanted me to give you a ride to the station." I gasp in shock, but the cop winks and leans closer to me to whisper, "He also said something about you coming alone and not bringing your posse with you."

I grin and step outside, shutting the door behind me. "Let's go." I should have known it wasn't going to be that easy. As the cop car backs out of the driveway, I turn to look at Noel's house and see the front door fly open. Betty rushes out with Jack close on her heels.

We're halfway to the police station before the cop notices anything amiss. He looks into the rearview mirror and startles. "What the…"

I look around and see Jack driving Ally's car behind us. Apparently there wasn't any time to find another vehicle as the entire gang is piled into Ally's boat of a car. I laugh and wave to Ally and Betty, who are sharing the front bench seat with Jack. They wave back with huge smiles on their faces, their eyes bright with excitement.

My escort and I slip into the station via the back entry before Jack manages to find a parking place. I'm sure it's only a matter of time before the ladies assault the station, though. I'm ushered into an interrogation room where Noel is waiting for me.

I'm nervous and a bit tongue-tied when I look at him. This is the first time I've cast my eyes on him since he said he loved me. It becomes clear that now is not the time to get into lovey-dovey questions when Noel stands and ushers me to take a seat. He's all business.

"Piers Anderson has admitted to ransacking your house." He looks up at me to gauge my reaction. I just nod for him to continue. "We don't know why, but we think he's obsessed with you." I gasp, but Noel doesn't slow down. "There's obviously more to the story. We need to find a way to pressure him. To break him. Find his weak points."

I have no idea where Noel is going with this. "What do you want from me?"

Noel takes a deep breath before answering. "We want you to point him out in a line-up."

I scrunch my nose in confusion. "For what?"

Noel stares into my eyes as he answers. "I'm just putting the pieces together myself, but I think he's been following you for some time." I continue to stare at Noel in confusion. Wouldn't I know if someone was following me? Wouldn't I notice him? The only time I felt like someone was following me was after the will reading.

Noel grabs my hands. "Think, Izzy. Your house trashed, the car chase, the snooping around Anderson's house. What did you see every time?"

I just continue to stare at Noel. Something is nudging at my subconscious, but I can't bring the thought forward into my consciousness.

Noel waits. "Come on. Maybe when you see him, the final piece of the puzzle will fit in place."

I stare at Noel a moment longer before I reach for his hand. "Okay, let's do this."

Noel leads me to another room with a large mirror covering one wall and no furniture. He points to the mirror and I can see into another room. "Five men will file into the room. I need you to pick out the one who has been following you." He squeezes my shoulder. "They can't see you, so don't worry." I nearly laugh. Of course, they can't see me.

Noel nods to the other officer in the room. The officer leans forward and flips an intercom switch. "We're ready," he says, and I can hear the words echoed in the interrogation room where yet another officer is standing. He opens the door and the first man files into the room.

He has dirty blond hair and I immediately recognize him as another police officer. I turn to Noel and smile at him. He shrugs and whispers into my ear. "We need five men to make a line-up so…"

I turn away from Noel as another man enters the interrogation room. He has blond hair like his predecessor, but it's a lighter color and when the two men stand together I notice they're nearly the same height as well. I have no idea who this man is. I shake my head.

The third man enters and my breath leaves me. Shocking white hair – I know this man. I walk closer to the mirror and stare at him. His eyes bore into me as if he can see through the two-way mirror. Eyes so dark they look like pure evil. I can't look away, mesmerized by the devil himself. Noel shakes my shoulder to get my attention.

"Do you know him?"

I nod. "Yeah. I bumped into him at the law firm." I try to think back to other times I felt eyes upon me. "I think he may have been following me since the first time I went to the law firm." I close my eyes and think of the other incidents. I gasp as I remember the blur of white hair in the car outside my house after I came home to find my door open. The car was a Chevy Impala, the same car that followed us from Ajax Mining. I nearly collapse, but Noel steadies me.

"It's him, isn't it?" He asks.

I nod. "Yeah." Then I tell him about all the incidents when I saw a blur of white, which I now know is Anderson's unusual hair color.

After Noel finishes writing notes, he snaps his notebook shut and squeezes my shoulders. "Technically we have to finish the line-up." I nod and watch as two more men file into the room. I don't recognize them.

"What now?" I ask Noel as the men shuffle out of the opposite room.

"Now," he says with a smile. "The fun begins." He gives me a quick peck on the cheek before leaving the room. The other officer escorts me to the front desk area where the gang's waiting. We're given strict orders to wait in this area before the officer disappears.

Jack rushes to me as soon as we are alone. "What's going on?" I fill him and the ladies in on super creepy stalker guy before settling in for the wait.

It quickly feels like we've been waiting hours for something to happen. A peek at the clock shows that's it's actually only been the longest hour of my life. I stand and stretch my muscles. I'm desperate for action. I walk over to the receptionist. "Do you have a soda machine or something?"

"Yeah," she nods. "It's in the break room. It's for personnel only but go on back." She points me to the left. I walk slowly trying to make the simple task of getting a Coke take as long as possible. A door opens as I walk past and two officers shuffle out.

"YOU!" a man yells, and I stop. "YOU!" he yells again, and I can't help but turn my face toward the sound. Piers Anderson is standing in the room that the officers just vacated. His evil eyes are focused on me. Everyone in the station is frozen. Anderson takes advantage of the distraction his yelling has created and runs around the table rushing towards me. I'm immobilized – a deer caught in headlights. At the last moment, Noel runs forward and tackles Anderson to the ground.

"You ruined everything," Anderson screams as Noel knees him in his back and reaches for his handcuffs. "I could have made millions off that old bitch's property." Noel has him handcuffed now and hauls him to his feet.

I momentarily lose control of my actions as his words make me see red. "How dare you call my grandma a bitch?" I yell just as an officer grabs me before I can reach Anderson. I raise my hand, prepared to slap Anderson, but the officer reaches forward and snatches my hand.

There are not enough officers in this station, let alone Oklahoma, to stop my lady posse, however. They are marching straight for Anderson, bags raised in preparation. Betty reaches Anderson first. She hits him square in the stomach with her bag.

I hear a large oomph and Anderson doubles over. Betty looks him up and down. "You need to respect your elders, young man."

Jack is quicker than the cops who are standing still staring at Betty. He grabs her and pulls her away from Anderson. A moment of silence follows before Betty's entourage begins to clap. The room fills with masculine chuckles as Anderson fumes. Noel takes him back into the interrogation room and slams the door. Betty takes a bow before we return to the front desk to wait yet again.

Another two hours pass before we see Noel again. He walks straight to me and crushes me in a tight hug. "You're safe," he whispers into my hair. "You're safe."

I push a bit so I can look up at his face. "Of course I'm safe."

He shakes his head. "You don't understand." He runs a hand down his face. "The ransacked house, the car chase." He moans. "Fuck, I've been out of my mind."

Wow, I've been a complete idiot. Too blind to see what's in front of me. While I was worried about whether Noel really liked me and acting like a hormone-crazed teenager, he was out of his mind with worry about my safety. I can't believe I missed it. Even now, he has dark circles under his eyes. I face plant into Noel's very capable chest.

Our tender moment is of course interrupted by the Ben-Gay crew and Jack. Jack clears his throat, but Betty isn't much on being discreet. "What's going on?" She asks without so much as a how do you do.

"I've still got some paperwork to fill out," he raises his hands for quiet when the ladies start to bristle with indignation. "Don't worry. I'll tell you everything that's going on. Can we meet at my house in say, an hour?" He asks as his stomach growls loudly.

Ally jumps up. "Let's go," she says in a pushy voice I'm not used to hearing come from her. "Noel hasn't eaten all day. We'll just have time to prepare something."

I give Noel a quick kiss. "See you in an hour."

He hugs me close before reluctantly letting me go. "An hour, my love." He turns and walks back into the bowels of the police station.

Chapter 35

"The End" by The Doors

The ladies rush around Noel's kitchen preparing a feast fit for a king. I'm setting the table when I hear the roar of a GTO in the driveway. I hurry to the kitchen door and fling it open in time to see Noel get out of his car and start to saunter toward me. Now here's a predator I wouldn't mind catching his prey – as long as his prey is me, that is. I run to him and jump into his outstretched arms.

Betty tuts and tells us to get a move on. She insists that we feed Noel before he fills us in. Everyone agrees, but their agreement is obviously reluctant as five old ladies and one man shovel food into their mouths at a rate a Japanese food competitor would be proud of.

When the coffee is brewed and the pie plated, Noel begins his story. "As you already discovered, Piers Franklin Ajax Anderson worked at Ajax Mining. His uncle, Alex Ajax, fired him when they discovered Anderson was bullying landowners into selling their mineral rights to Ajax Mining."

"They just fired him?" I ask, angry at Alex Ajax and his treatment of Jack and I all over again. "What about the landowners and the harassment? What did they do about that?"

"I talked to Ajax Mining. They settled all of the harassment cases out of court and made everyone sign confidentiality clauses," Noel explains.

"He could have freaking told us!"

Noel shakes his head. "Ajax Mining is a multi-billion dollar business for a reason. They're not spending any money if they don't have to."

"Anyway," Betty's impatient. "Back to the story."

Noel continues his explanation. "Without a job, he ran through his trust fund in no time. It seems Mr. Anderson has a bit of a gambling problem. He still had access to Ajax Mining through his family though, and he stole some maps, which indicated where Ajax Mining was considering buying mineral rights. He started going after landowners – acting like he was still an employee of Ajax Mining. Anna was, unfortunately, one of his targets." He takes a deep breath before continuing. "He investigated Anna, and thought she had no living relatives to stand up for her." He smiles sadly at me.

"Technically, she didn't. We aren't related by blood," I feel the need to clarify.

Noel shakes his head at me. "Family doesn't always mean blood," he whispers to me before continuing louder for the rest of the gang. "Anyway, he thought he could bully Anna into giving him the mineral rights."

I hear several snorts of disbelief. "Not bloody likely," Jack says.

"When Anna told Anderson she'd saved the land by putting an easement on it, he went totally bonkers and killed her."

"But how?" Betty wants to know, as do I.

"He injected her with air."

Gasp. "That really works?" I ask.

Noel nods. "It's not as easy as it sounds, but it does work." Not as easy as it sounds? I shiver. I don't want to think about poor Grandma fighting off a madman. Noel squeezes me. "She was asleep and didn't suffer," he whispers to me.

"Asleep? In the middle of the day?" I find that hard to believe.

"Not the middle of the day." Noel gives me a knowing look. "Anderson came back at night when she was sleeping. He claims she didn't wake."

"If her arthritis was bothering her, she'd take a sleeping pill," Ally confirms.

"So Grandma was really murdered?" Jack slumps against the wall. "I always thought it was just malarkey."

"What?" I nearly jump out of my seat.

Jack shrugs. "I've had a ball investigating, but I thought it was just a game."

"You need a boyfriend," I announce and he blushes.

"Anyway," Betty's anxious for Noel to continue the story. "And then what?"

"First, he waited. He assumed the land would come up for public auction when Anna died. Just to be sure, he staked out the lawyer's office." He turns to me.

"And that's when he discovered me and started stalking me." I shiver in recollection.

Noel holds me tight. "He didn't know what was going on, but he figured you were his best chance. He ransacked your house to search for your files and to find out what had happened with the land. He didn't discover anything and started stalking you full-time." I full-body shiver. "He freaked when you went to Ajax Mining."

"He just confessed all this?" Seems odd to me.

"We had a lot of leverage." Noel smiles at me. "We caught him red-handed at your house and then you identified him as your stalker. We were pushing him hard in interrogation and not getting anywhere when you happened to walk by, and he went after you." Noel turns to me. "Don't ever do that again, by the way." I shrug. I didn't do anything – not on purpose anyway. "After he attacked you and shouted about making millions from Anna's property, it wasn't hard to pressure him to confess."

"So it's over," Betty sounds disappointed.

"Mr. Anderson is going to be locked up for a very long time." I sag against Noel in relief.

The ladies gather their things and say their goodbyes. Betty looks upset, but her gang is obviously relieved. Jack kisses me good-bye and then it's just Noel and I.

"What now?" I ask. Noel throws me over his shoulder and heads to the bedroom in response.

Epilogue

"Happy" by Natasha Bedingfield

"I got it," I hear Noel yell as the doorbell rings.

I'm in the kitchen preparing the lemonade the ladies drink as if it's going out of style. I make a huge batch of 'adult' lemonade for the ladies who aren't driving and a smaller pitcher for the designated drivers. They rotate who drives because otherwise the whining and complaining is never ending.

After we had recovered from Grandma's murder and the whole stalking thing, things calmed down. Noel and I decided to move in together. Although it didn't exactly go like that. Basically, Noel ordered me to move in with him or else he was going to move in with me. I didn't get much choice in the matter. Not that I'm complaining, mind you.

Although we liked our houses, we realized that we loved Grandma's. We sold both of our homes and used the money to bring Grandma's place into the current century. All the bathrooms have been updated, and we added an ensuite bathroom to the master bedroom. Noel put a man cave in the basement where he and Jack spend entirely too much time. Luckily, I'm allowed in the man cave although frou-frou drinks have been banned. Geesh. You try one time to use your new martini glasses.

Noel is still working as a detective with the local police force, but I'm no longer doing graphic work. Between the money I made from selling my house and Grandma's bank accounts, I don't need to ever work again. I'm not one to stay still, though. I volunteer for Save the Plains and I'm thinking about starting a no-kill animal shelter. Whenever I bring up my plans for the shelter, Noel just shakes his head and laughs. I'll show him.

I hear Betty laughing in the sunroom, which is prepared for today's knitting group meeting. Jack, Noel, and I are pretty attached to the old lady gang. When Ally asked if they could continue to hold knitting group meetings at our house, I didn't hesitate to say yes. Not a lot of knitting happens, but the gossiping is endless. Noel has even used information from the ladies to help him with background information on suspects.

Don't tell the ladies though. They'll pester him to help all the time.

Ally walks into the kitchen holding a Tupperware cake taker. I smile in anticipation. "Hi Ally," I reach over to kiss her cheek. "What did you bring today?" All the ladies spoil us with pies and cakes when they come over.

"Ta da!" she shouts as she opens the Tupperware. Awesome! My favorite chocolate cake, but wait, she only makes this for special occasions.

"What are you up to?" I ask with my hands on my hips – all kinds of untrusting.

She blushes, but shakes her head. "Nothing."

Yeah right, I think, but manage to keep my mouth shut. These ladies are immune to my interrogation techniques so I let it go and grab the tray of lemonade and glasses, and walk to the sunroom. Betty, Rosemary, Martha, and Rose are already seated, their knitting bags unopened on the floor. I pour lemonade for everyone.

Ally walks in with slices of chocolate cake. Noel and Jack are on her heels. Noel hands me a piece of cake and smiles at me. "Yum!" I say and grab my fork to immediately dive in.

Shit. I bite down on something hard. I reach in my mouth to pull out whatever the offensive object is. What in the world? Is that a ring? I look up startled to see Noel down on one knee in front of me. The ladies are quiet for a change.

Noel clears his throat. "Izzy, would you make me the happiest man on earth by agreeing to be my wife?"

This has to be the corniest marriage proposal ever and I love it. "Yes!" I shout and jump up from my chair to tackle Noel. The ladies and Jack clap. I don't care if we have an audience. My mouth locks on Noel. If he's lucky, I'll let him up for air after our first anniversary.

Thanks!

Thanks for reading *Murder, Mystery & Dating Mayhem*. Show an indie writer some love and write a review. I also need to thank all my friends and family that have helped and supported me along the way. You rock! This version was edited by my gal pal Carol Allen. Thanks for being a sweetie pie and professional to boot! Oh wait, I think I forgot someone – my hubby. Thanks to my husband for putting up with me jumping out of bed in the middle of the night to take notes, dripping water everywhere when I run from the shower with a great idea, and acting like my characters are real people (although he totally gets into that – What's Izzy up to today he asks every day when he gets home).

A Note about the Environment

Save the Plains is not an existing environmental group, although there are several groups with similar names. I just liked the sound of the name. The group is based upon The Nature Conservancy, which does have a branch in Oklahoma. The Nature Conservancy has indeed saved thousands upon thousands of acres of land from development, whether by fracking or otherwise. You can find out more about them about www.nature.org.

I'm not going to try and convince you that fracking is wrong. Lord knows once I start arguing it's hard to get me to shut up. But I will say one thing. How much of the earth do we have to use up and abuse before we realize that we only have one earth?

About the Author – Me

I was born and raised in Wisconsin but think I'm a European. After spending my senior year of high school in Germany, I developed a bad case of wanderlust that is yet to be cured. After high school I returned to the U.S. to go to college ending up with a Bachelor's degree in History at the tender age of twenty while still managing to spend time bouncing back and forth to Europe during vacations. Unable to find a job after college and still suffering from wanderlust, I joined the U.S. Army as a Military Policewoman for five years. While stationed in

Heidelberg, Germany, I met my future husband, a flying – literally – Dutchman. After being given my freedom from the Army, I went off to law school. I finished law school and moved to the Netherlands with my husband and became a commercial lawyer for more than a decade. During a six-month break from the lawyering world, I wrote my first book, *Unforeseen Consequences*. Although I finished the book, I went back to the law until I could no longer take it and upped stakes and moved to Germany to start a B&B. Three years after starting the B&B, I got the itch to try something new and decided to pull the manuscript for *Unforeseen Consequences* out of the attic and get it published as an e-book. Deciding that I may have indeed finally found what I want to do with my life, I went on to write *Buried Appearances*. After moving to Istanbul, I wrote *Life Discarded*. Feeling pressured by my girlfriends to write a chick lit novel, I tried my hand at humor with *Murder, Mystery & Dating Mayhem*. Between tennis, running, traveling, singing off tune, drinking entirely too many adult drinks, and reading books like they are going out of style, I write articles for a local expat magazine and various websites, review other indie authors' books, write a blog about whatever comes to mind and am working on my fifth book.

Other books by D.E. Haggerty:

Unforeseen Consequences

Buried Appearances

Life Discarded

CPSIA information can be obtained
at www.ICGtesting.com
Printed in the USA
LVHW080729161222
735349LV00014B/443

9 781508 574699